A Spell Behind Bars

A *fantabulous* tale
by
Bowvayne

With *delisherous* drawings
by Alan Snow

*To the walker of the butterfly path.
You made childhood sparkle.*

First published in the UK in 2004 by Usborne Publishing Ltd.,
Usborne House, 83-85 Saffron Hill, London EC1N 8RT, England.
www.usborne.com

A catalogue record for this title is available
from the British Library.

JFMAMJJA OND/06

ISBN 0 7460 6028 9

Printed in India.

Contents

The following is based on some untidy jottings left by Cyril Spectre in Bowvayne's writing room.

Chapter 1

A Pain in the Backside

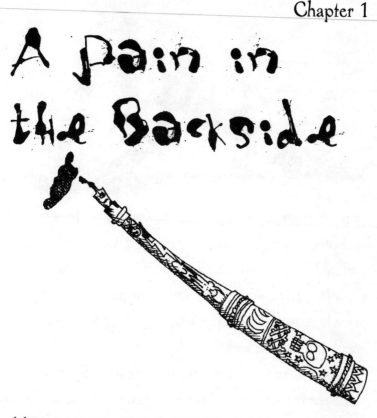

"PHEW! WHAT A STENCH!" said Danny Cloke, trying to pick up an old piece of carpet – matted with hair, and stained with food, dried-on ribbons of hyena slobber and things far worse – without actually having to touch it. Danny was helping his dad clear out the garage where the laughing hyena, Cuddles, had lived

until a month ago. The hyena belonged to Danny's real-life, twenty-first-century wicked stepmother, Aunt Mildred. But thankfully she had left now, and the vicious Cuddles had gone with her…or, to be precise, it had gone after her, as in *chased* after her, mistaking her for its next meal. But that's another story.

Once, Danny had been an ordinary boy. He could trace the beginnings of his weird topsy-turvy life back to when he was seven years old and his mother had left home to look for the world's rarest bird, the Venezuelan Long-tailed Pink Polka-dotted Home-wrecking Cuckoo. He hadn't ever seen her again.

Almost immediately afterwards, Aunt Mildred had come onto the scene; and she had overwhelmed Danny's life like a great cloud of dark, poisonous smoke. The fact that she was now gone too was a matter for great celebration. And Danny didn't think it likely that Dad would have her back after he'd discovered that she'd been feeding his son food from the hyena's bowl, forcing him to sit in broom cupboards and ripping up letters from his absent mother, among other shocking crimes. Since Aunt Mildred's hasty retreat, Danny had entered the most blissful period he could remember since Mum was around and that was nearly four years ago. There'd been a trip to the zoo (where Dad had got into trouble for feeding the elephant a peanut) and the movies (where Dad had come up trumps again by screaming out loud during the scary bit), and drives in the countryside. At the funfair they'd driven the dodgem cars and been on the big dipper, and succeeded in getting lost in the haunted house, as well. But it wasn't even eating all his favourite foods that was the highlight for Danny – it was the laughter that they'd shared.

Danny thought he was safe now and life couldn't be better. And today Dad had promised a barbecue for them and some friends when they finished this smelly chore.

Now, Danny and his dad went in and out of the garage's side door, carrying tea-chests, old newspapers, blankets, bowls – in fact anything the hyena had ever licked, nibbled or slobbered on – and they threw it all on a bonfire that was well ablaze in the back garden.

"Yuck! This stinks!" Danny exclaimed again. In spite of his complaints he was secretly pleased that the last vestiges of Aunt Mildred's terrible reign were going up in flames.

It was late Saturday morning. Danny licked his lips when he thought of the promised barbecue: Dad's sausages, piping hot and covered in tomato sauce all wrapped up in a slice of white bread; and the way he did those deliciously soft, moist chicken breasts with the crispy skin so close to being burned, but not quite. They were so much better than Aunt Mildred's meals. When she had bothered to feed him anything at all, the best he could expect was a rotten egg sprayed with perfume to disguise the terrible smell. Or stale bread rolls with hyena-hair filling, and sometimes, for a special treat, a blob of mayonnaise, liberally sprinkled with dead flies.

Danny heaved the foul carpet onto the bonfire and

turned to get the next load. His dad was bent over, struggling with some newspaper stuck to the garage floor. "Get me something to scrape this up with, Danny," he called out over his shoulder.

As Danny stared at his dad's backside, an odd feeling came over him. It was as if the world had tilted slightly and the reds and yellows and blues and greens had drained out of it and some hitherto unimagined, but horrible new colours had been tipped in. He shook his head from side to side to clear the vision.

Suddenly he heard an evil cackling laugh. Beside him, Danny saw an ugly, goblin-like creature, as insubstantial as mist. His heart gave a terrible lurch. The creature had nine curly, pointed little tails, a mighty hooked nose, and a horrible, staring, gimlet-eyed look. Its overall appearance was one of deepest wickedness.

Although frightened out of his wits, Danny's mind dully registered that his dad was shouting. "Hurry up! Let's get this finished. Our guests will be here in half an hour." Dad was bent over still, his bottom sticking right up in the air.

His fright forgotten, Danny began sniggering. His

dad's backside made a good, plump target. He had an overwhelming desire to kick it. He didn't know where the feeling had come from. He wasn't normally the sort of boy to go around kicking his father up the backside, or even to think of it, but something seemed to have taken control of his mind. He couldn't help himself.

"What are you doing back there?" bellowed his dad. "Fetch me the wallpaper stripper from the top shelf, would you?"

A dizzying whirligig of strange, alien colours and far-off echoing laughter overwhelmed Danny's normal senses.

I don't believe it, thought Danny to himself, blinking furiously. But I can *see* it! He's stuck a target on the back of his trousers! It says "Kick the bull's-eye to win the prize!" There's a big, fat sign for a hundred smackers in the middle of his big, fat backside!

"Danny!" yelled Dad, his bottom doing a provocative wiggle.

"All right!" roared Danny. "If that's what you want, that's what you're going to get!" He gave his father's bum a tremendous boot, the sort that would make a jackass proud.

"Woo-hoo! One hundred! Hand over the money, Dad."

The instant Danny had done it, he glimpsed the wicked creature again. A moment later it had vanished before his eyes.

Now, if a grizzly bear had woken from its winter hibernation to find Danny in its cave finishing its last jar of honey and wearing its favourite slippers, it wouldn't be as angry as Danny's dad was then.

Eventually, after Mr. Cloke had exhausted himself yelling, Danny was sent to his room for the rest of the day. He was in total disgrace, the worst he'd ever known. Dad also rang Mrs. Falconer, the mother of Danny's friend Imogen (the new girl in his class at school) and cancelled the barbecue, promising that they could come around some other time "when Danny stops behaving so childishly".

What made the whole business even more awful, Danny reflected, wasn't so much that the sun was shining and he was banished up here, or that Dad was limping around the garden with a sandwich in one hand and clutching his buttocks with the other, or that the barbecue wasn't being fired up. It was what he'd heard

Dad mutter under his breath as Danny climbed the stairs to begin his punishment that really worried him.

"I was warned that you would try and kick me up the backside, but I dismissed it as rubbish. It seems I was wrong…" And he gave Danny a frosty look. The words had chilled Danny to the marrow of his bones.

Who on earth would warn Dad about getting a kick up the bum? Danny wondered. It was crazy. Perhaps it was Aunt Mildred. But how would she know he'd do something like that? Danny had tried to ask his dad who'd said such a thing, but Dad angrily refused to be drawn further.

Sitting alone in his room, the hours passed slowly and it began to get dark. Danny knew his dad wasn't likely to change his mind about banishing him up here, so with a sigh of hopelessness, he took off his shirt and jeans and lifted his pillow to retrieve his pyjamas. Then he remembered he'd put them in the laundry basket downstairs that morning. His fresh pair would be in the airing cupboard, next door to Dad's bedroom – and the floorboards along the landing were prone to squeak. What was he going to do now? If he was caught wandering about outside his room, it might stir his dad up again, so Danny just put on his dressing gown.

Then he crawled under his bed; a place of refuge during Aunt Mildred's time, when he'd sought to escape her and to hide his treasures. Now it felt like somewhere safe again, safe from whatever had come over him outside; and from that evil creature he'd seen. It was a creepy feeling to think you were no longer the master of your own actions, and, perhaps, that someone else was. He thought about it all again for the hundredth time.

I wouldn't even do *that* to Chopper Chowdhury, thought Danny. And I can't think of a kid at school that I hate more. To kick my own father so hard up the... up the... Oh, the shame of it.

He sighed heavily again and looked at his Cyril Spectre books lined up in order against the wall under the bed, front covers facing him. He had hidden them under here to stop Aunt Mildred discovering the outlawed books. Aunt Mildred was a staunch fan of Cyril Clegg's ghastly tomes, such as *Skipping to the Sewing-Machine Shop with my Aunt Betty* and *The Fine Art of Cutting*

Lawns with Nail Scissors. She hated Cyril Spectre's books and threatened to burn any she found.

Absently, Danny picked up the final book in the row and opened it. He read the title page aloud, "*A Turn in the Grave*, by…"

Suddenly he stopped. Something on the page had shimmered bright gold. Was it a trick of the light? He stared at the page. Then he gasped as a golden envelope materialized out of nowhere.

The envelope was addressed to him and in the top right-hand corner was a single gleaming image of a silver palm tree on a tiny desert island. From the middle of the palm's trunk, majestic, swan-like wings sprouted. Next to this, the envelope was postmarked "Paradise".

"Cyril Spectre!" Danny shouted excitedly as he tore open the letter. The ghostly writer who'd helped him get rid of Aunt Mildred was the only person (that is, to say, *spirit*) he knew in Paradise.

ATTENTION: Danny Cloke
45 Sting Close
Nettle Bottom
Wessex
WX1 0UCH

Twelfth day of April

Dear Danny,

The fact that you can read the dirling, swazzling spirit ink with which this misterpiece is wrotten means that someone has placed a Zero Hex upon you. The hex will make you act in such disgusterous ways that very soon you'll be even more unpompular than Lady Ponsonby the day she went to the races, mistaking a phewsome skunk for her fashionable hat.

Anyway, I have managed to get permission from Paradise's S.A.I.N.T.s (governors of the Soul And Internal Naughtiness Tribunal) to warn you of this impending disaster.

A human can only place a Zero Hex upon you

17

with the assistance of one of our mortal enemies, the Hobblegobs of Gloom. Let me assure you, it's irklesome indeed to be endlessly parrying these pugnant poltroons when we could be perambulating in Paradise instead.

Despite our feud, residents of Paradise, known as Haloes, are normally strictly forbidden from interfering in earthly concerns. But due to my magnifantabulous services to children I've been made a S.A.I.N.T. and have persuaded the rest of the governors that you are an exceptional case.

Anyway, this is the all-important bit. Read this carefully and do exactly as instructed to avert the baddlesome magic of the Zero Hex. Later this morning you will be outside with your father, helping him clean up. At 11.46 a.m. you will feel a sudden, inexplicable desire to kick your father up the bottom. Immediately you have this pathetiful desire, shout "A RIPE PONGULESCENCE!" at the top of your voice. I know it sounds silly, but you'll have your hands full of stinksome, festerfying Cuddles carpet and your dad will just think you're messing around. These words WILL break the Zero Hex. Once the Zero Hex is averted, my superior, Saint Bernard, will deduce who the scumbletons are that initiated it and why.

Failure to follow these instructions will mean that you'll kick your father up the backside and the Zero Hex will be unleashed. Then, unless you can discover in time who the human and the Hobblegob are who have plotted against you to create the Zero Hex between them, and then find out how to destroy it, the hex will end with you having A SPELL BEHIND BARS.

Your friend,
CYRIL
(Trainee Miracle Worker, S.A.I.N.T.)

If Danny hadn't already been lying down, he would probably have collapsed on the floor by now. Just when his life seemed to be getting back to normal, someone had put a hex on him. A Zero Hex. Danny had seen what hexes could do. After all, that's how he and Cyril had got rid of Aunt Mildred. Danny gulped as he remembered the terrible things that had happened to her: the purple hair, the beard, the smell that had driven Cuddles wild, her arrest by the police…

Danny knew he was in deep trouble.

Chapter 2

Dog Collared

CYRIL MUST HAVE MADE some sort of mistake, thought Danny, and the letter had arrived too late. The Zero Hex was unleashed. What else would it make him do? Whatever it was, it was going to make him as *unpompular* as someone wearing a skunk on their head; that much he did know. Danny's mind boggled.

Unless he discovered the perpetrators of the hex and destroyed the pact between them, he would end up having "a spell behind bars".

What did that mean, precisely? It sounded horribly like he would be going to prison. But he'd been fooled by this sort of wordplay before. Once, he'd thought he was going to lose his Cyril Spectre books but, even worse, it'd turned out that he might lose his family. It had all ended well, but Danny couldn't bear to go through the terror of something like that again. Especially now that he and his dad had become so close, and he was receiving letters regularly from his mum.

His only chance of escape was to discover who had placed the hex on him. Danny wondered who could do such a thing, and decided that only Aunt Mildred could be this devious and this cruel. But how had she been able to contact the Hobblegobs of Gloom? Aunt Mildred was certainly evil. But that didn't mean she had access to the spirit realm. He remembered the foul creature cackling at him when that weird feeling had come over him in the garden. Had that been a Hobblegob?

Danny didn't know how to track down Aunt Mildred,

let alone a Hobblegob. And even then he'd have to break the Zero Hex. How on earth was he going to do that? His heart sank as he imagined finally hunting down Aunt Mildred and the Hobblegob to some horrible, midnight churchyard full of broken headstones, and asking politely if they'd mind calling the whole thing off. No, that just wouldn't work.

The letter faded into nothingness before his eyes, and Danny pondered his fate.

He was left with just his books again. Even now they were a comfort to him. His eyes scanned across the titles:

1. Witches' Brew
2. The Space-Shuttle Vacuum Cleaner
3. A Dragon of an Aunt Done Medium-Rare
4. Our Old School Deadmaster
5. Horace: The Teacher's Pet Who
Hopped with Bities
6. Mind the Step, Mother
7. A Turn in the Grave

"The greatest writer in the entire history of the

universe," Danny said to himself, pulling his dressing gown tightly around his neck. Wanting to take his mind off all the momentous events of the day, he picked a book from the middle of the row and read from a page at random.

The old school deadmaster fixed the little girl with a squinty, flinty, beady, greedy eye. He reached into his coffin for his ivory cane, the cane that would make her the same as him...

Dead!

"I don't care about me any more," cried Jade. "Now the whole world knows what you are!"

When he touched the cane the deadmaster pulled his fingers back sharply as if they'd been burned. There was a *swazzling dirl* of magic about him. "No!" he screamed.

The great Rainbow Bubble was back! It picked the deadmaster up, holding him within it, and an instant later hurled him into the deepest darkest *dunksome* water of the *pongulescent* sewage farm.

"Help! Help!" he wailed in alarm. "I can't swim! I can't swi...glug glug...sw...glu...p."

Danny found himself smiling for the first time since that morning. As well as the amazing language Cyril used, he loved the way the villains in the stories always came to a sticky end. He went to the back of the book to read the message from the author.

With the exception of Cyril's final book, *A Turn in the Grave*, the message at the back of his books was always the same. After all that had happened last month, Danny looked upon the message as a personal note from an old friend. It read:

P.S. Don't ever write to me unless you want to lose something dear to your heart, or you want a turn in the grave.

Under-the-Sod Publishers.

E-mail: <u>spectrehaunts@alcheeposuper.com</u>

Cyril Spectre had sold ten million books in seventy different languages in eighty-five countries and received letters from only one fan following this warning: Danny Cloke. And by writing his fan letter, despite the warning, Danny had unleashed wonderful wild magic.

Wonderful for Danny, that is, but the consequences had been devastating for his wicked stepmother. Cyril's hexes saw to it that Aunt Mildred had had a series of disasters culminating in her fleeing from the house with Cuddles in close pursuit. The final hex upon her was so strong she smelled like a sickly sack of rotten meat and, quite naturally, the hyena thought she was dinner.

It had soon become apparent to Danny that his favourite writer, Cyril Spectre, was formerly Cyril Clegg, the most boring children's writer ever and the country's founding member of a secret organization of child-haters called

S.L.A.Y. (the Society of Librarians Against Youth). Clegg's life had ended in the local Al Cheepo's supermarket when he was struck on the head by a falling box of frozen fish fingers. Cyril Clegg had only become Cyril Spectre after death. Instead of becoming a horrible Hobblegob or a high-flying Halo straight away, he had been transformed into one of those spirits who gets trapped in the waiting rooms of the Afterlife – he had become a Spectre. Still, at least Cyril had time then to write his wonderful children's books, to make up for the steaming cowpats of novels he'd written as Cyril Clegg.

Danny's eyes lingered on the front cover of Cyril's latest book. The others were works of fiction, but this one, *A Turn in the Grave*, was true and Danny was the star! He had read it every day since Aunt Mildred's departure.

As he lay under the bed, pondering the inexplicably odd events of the past weeks, a strange feeling came over Danny: the same feeling he'd experienced in the garden earlier. His world gave a weird diagonal lurch as if he were the seasick skipper of a little boat caught up in a storm. He caught a momentary glance of the same goblin-like creature stretched out beside him, and heard the same maniacal cackling.

Totally in the grip of the magic, Danny gathered up the seven Cyril Spectre books, then he rolled out from under the bed, opened his window and flung the first book onto the bonfire in the garden below. The bonfire was by now only a faint orange circle of dying embers, but it crackled and leaped into flames at this fresh offering. Tongues of fire licked the edges of the pages, curling them and turning them black. He flung the second book in an oddly jerky fashion, as if invisible strings controlled his arms. Then the third…a fourth…until all the books, including the priceless first copy of *A Turn in the Grave*, were ablaze. The ashes floated upwards before night consumed them.

Suddenly, Danny found himself panting like a dog. He got on his hands and knees and in an extraordinary motion that could only be described as a perky lumber, lumbered perkily out of his bedroom, downstairs, through the front door and into the street. Danny spotted the object of his desire – a lamp-post! He cocked his leg at it. His dressing gown fell open, revealing his underpants to the street. A man wearing a clerical dog collar walked by, goggling at him.

"Evening, Vicar," said the hexed Danny. The bald-headed vicar hurried past with a look of disgust on his face.

Then, Danny's world shifted again, and feeling himself returning to normal, his first thought was utter devastation that he'd destroyed his beloved Cyril Spectre books. When his wits returned properly, he wondered where he was, and was hideously embarrassed to find himself on his hands and knees with one leg in the air.

And even more horrified when he saw Dad watching him through the window, his face going redder by the second.

Chapter 3

Grave Concerns

ALTHOUGH DANNY WAS NUMBED by the loss of his beloved Cyril Spectre books, Dad didn't give him time to mourn the next day. Instead, Danny spent Sunday morning writing and rehearsing his speech of apology to Mr. Nannish, the local vicar. Dad, still fuming, paced up and down dictating the words, and

Danny didn't complain when he was made to rewrite it five times while Dad got it "absolutely right".

Just before lunchtime Danny cycled to Upon-the-Sod Church to make the speech in person. Dad had told him to enjoy the bicycle ride because afterwards he was going to be grounded for a month. Grounded for a month sounded like the holiday of a lifetime compared to a spell behind bars, Danny thought grimly. At least this chore was the perfect opportunity to visit Cyril's grave. He hoped that he would be able to contact Cyril to ask him how to stop the Zero Hex. Danny had said what he thought was a final goodbye to him when Cyril Spectre had left the waiting room to become a Halo in Paradise nearly a month ago, but now, he hoped his old friend might come back and help him get rid of the Zero Hex, despite the tone of finality in his letter. He could only hope.

Danny dismounted and wheeled his bicycle through the wooden gate at the rear of the church. Past an impressive holly bush, Danny paused before the grey marble gravestone he had visited often since Aunt Mildred's departure.

In fine gold filigree was written:

CYRIL CLEGG
Terminat hora
diem; terminat
author opus.

He remembered the time he had traced his finger around the letters "CYRIL CLEGG" and had fallen into a spirit realm somewhere below Cyril's grave. Overwhelmed with curiosity at the amazing, magical things that had happened before, Danny had tried it again several times since but that particular piece of magic seemed to have been extinguished.

"Your message didn't get through in time, Cyril," Danny said, addressing the gravestone. "Although I don't suppose it's like posting a letter to the next town," he added charitably. He stooped and uprooted a weed from the plot. "Don't know when I'll be allowed to come again. I can't even pass the time reading your books. The Zero Hex made me burn them. Is this hex Aunt Mildred's doing?" he said in sudden despair, slamming his fist on the cold stone of the grave.

Sparks flew at his touch, and Danny jumped back in surprise. Rubbing his hand, he stared at the surface of the gravestone, which was swirling and flickering like an old television set. There was a haze of static snow and then, to Danny's amazement, a picture began to form, and he could make out the image of a helicopter landing in a long, green valley.

The craft's two occupants were a scar-faced pilot, whom Danny was sure he recognized but he couldn't remember from where, and another figure, muffled up in a fur coat and hood.

Suddenly, the helicopter took off again and rapidly banked away as a baying pack of dogs moved in for the kill.

"Whew! That was a close one," Danny heard a crackly, distant voice say. "There's more and more of them every time. I don't know how much longer we can keep this up." A majestic snow-capped mountain loomed before them. "I'm going to take her right up to the summit, Boss. Give you time to contact Julius Rapax on the videophone. Then we'll have to think about refuelling again."

"Okay, Lopez," said a woman's voice.

Looking on, Danny was confused. The woman was about to contact someone with the same name as his school: Julius Rapax. He'd never actually thought that there might be a real Mr. Rapax. Maybe his school was named after this person.

The rapid take-off had caused the woman's hood to slip, revealing a completely bald head, tufts of bristles sprouting from her face and an extraordinary beard. It took Danny only a split second to recognize...Aunt Mildred!

Apart from the gleaming baldness, bristly tufts and long purple beard, she resembled an ape-like predecessor of humankind. As her hands reached to pull up the hood again, her coat fell open.

The pilot quickly adjusted his gas mask. "Please, Mildred. Close your coat, quick! It smells like a herd of sweaty goats!"

"All right! All right!" snarled Aunt Mildred. "Spare me the details. You know it's not me."

"One hundred dogs beg to differ," Lopez spluttered through his mask, his face turning battleship grey.

"Stop trying to be clever, Mr. Lopez. What I mean is that it's some sort of curse that's made me look and smell like this."

After a moment's silence the pilot spoke again. "Mildred, are you going to shave off your beard?" he suggested delicately. "Or at least give it a trim? Mr. Rapax is S.L.A.Y.'s world leader and the only multi-trillionaire in the world, after all."

"Haven't you noticed?" Aunt Mildred protested. "The more I cut it, the thicker and faster it grows back, and *grfffmmmm—*" The rest of her sentence was lost, as a sudden spurt from the errant beard saw it disappear into her mouth. Choking, she removed it again.

At that moment a videophone clipped onto the dashboard on the passenger's side hissed and crackled into life. A voice that was soft and ferocious at the same time, like the threatening rumble in the throat of a lion, said, "Hello, Mildred. Julius Rapax here."

Although the reception was poor, on the video-link, Danny could just make out a lithe man in a mask of finely beaten gold, wearing a white toga. The bare flesh of his arms and legs was deeply wrinkled, like an old elephant's skin.

"What are we going to do, Julius? See with your own eyes what Cyril has done to me," Aunt Mildred said, indicating her beard and face, her voice growing shriller by the second. "Cyril's supposed to be dead and he's supposed to be on our side…"

In the churchyard, a harsh woman's voice right beside Danny made him jump a metre in the air.

"Who's the nasty little brat? What's he staring at?"

Spinning around quickly, Danny saw an elderly lady with deep wrinkles and a long hooked nose. Her skin had the ghastly translucent appearance of rain clouds.

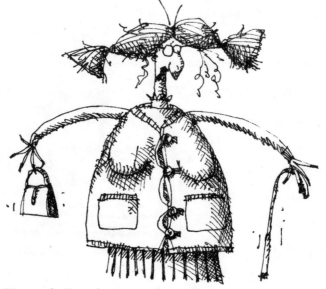

"I'm a fr-friend of Cyril's. And who are you?" Danny demanded defiantly, fright suddenly replaced by annoyance and frustration. He looked back at the images. They must have appeared for a reason; he was meant to watch them, and now this old crone had interrupted and he might miss something vital.

"I can't believe this!" The woman looked down her nose

at him. "I'm Malicia. I was Cyril's wife. He wouldn't have liked one of *you* here."

"One of whom?" Danny asked, without looking away from Cyril's gravestone where the images continued to flicker. He wished she would go away.

"He wouldn't have liked a *child* at his grave!" she said, shuddering at the word "child" as if it was something particularly odious. "*Especially you.*"

Especially me, Danny wondered. How did she even know him?

Quivering with suspicion, Danny looked at her again. His stomach turned over as he spotted that each of the buttons on her grey knitted cardigan said "S.L.A.Y." on it in blood-red letters.

"Go away, freak!" snapped Malicia.

But Danny was ignoring her, watching the images on the gravestone. Suddenly, they flickered and disappeared. "Come back!" he yelled.

Malicia looked at him, alarmed. "You're communing with this gravestone?" she said, and hurried off as if she had just realized she was in the company of a dangerous maniac.

Danny kneeled before Cyril's gravestone, cursing. Then something occurred to him. "That's it," he muttered as he watched Malicia Clegg beat a hasty retreat. "Aunt Mildred's still fighting off Cyril Spectre's hexes, so she's got her pals from S.L.A.Y. to spy on me to see whether I contact Cyril. That's all I need!"

Of all the incredible things Danny had discovered since his adventures began, it was S.L.A.Y. that made him most uneasy. The spirit realm seemed somehow lofty and distant compared to the everyday, in-this-world, here-and-now wickedness of S.L.A.Y.

Cyril had told him about this child-hating society. He had shamefacedly admitted that when he'd inhabited the mortal world as the living author Cyril Clegg, he'd sought to squash the life spark out of youngsters by writing the most boring children's books ever. The principal aim of S.L.A.Y., he confessed, was to find as many means as possible to turn children into boring, grey adults. Later, Danny had been shocked to learn that Aunt Mildred was the country's current president of S.L.A.Y.

He was struck by how bold it was for Malicia Clegg to wear S.L.A.Y. buttons in the street. Surely such an organization was illegal. And yet Malicia was parading about wearing her buttons.

Although he hadn't realized the significance of the initials at the time, Danny remembered Aunt Mildred wearing a brooch on her cardigan that said "Swanbourne Lake's Association of Yachtswomen". Maybe S.L.A.Y. was growing in strength and numbers every day and with it came a growing confidence.

There was something especially terrifying about Malicia Clegg. Danny couldn't put his finger on it, but it was more than just her ugly face.

But if Malicia was working for Aunt Mildred, then Danny saw a chance to do a little spying of his own. He had to find out whether Aunt Mildred was behind the Zero Hex, and Malicia might provide some clues. He decided to follow her.

As Danny wheeled his bicycle along the side of the church, he passed the entrance. He groaned. He'd forgotten all about the apologetic speech that he had to make to the vicar, his mind consumed as it was with the hex and the threat of a spell behind bars. There was the vicar now, his bald head bobbing up and down by the front gate as he said goodbye to worshippers leaving his Sunday morning service.

Danny recognized the reedy back of his teacher, Miss Snodgrass, as she disappeared down the street. He saw that Malicia Clegg was with her.

With a mixture of impatience and embarrassment, Danny approached the vicar, who was listening to a young couple. "Poor Alfie got me my first job," the great oaf of a man was saying to the vicar.

"Can't believe he's gone," added the woman. "A terrible business. A big cat, wasn't it?" There was something unpleasantly familiar about her; something about the hunching of the shoulders, the low-slung arms and the close-together eyes, that gave her a greedy, calculating look.

"Alfie Stringfellow's gone to a better place now, Blodwyn," said the vicar.

This was a surprising turn of events, thought Danny. Alfie Stringfellow was the school's horrid caretaker. Ever since Danny had heard of S.L.A.Y. he was sure that the revolting old codger must belong to it because of all the appalling things he'd done over the years. During P.E.

classes and on school sports days the sprinkler systems came on so often, drenching everyone, that he just had to have been doing it on purpose. And every so often, when you flushed any of the toilets around the school – and there was never any warning when it would happen – a jet of water would shoot out from the bowl straight into your eye. Two Year Fives had caught Mr. Stringfellow tampering with the toilets once and reported him to the principal, but nothing was done about it.

"String Bean", as he was secretly nicknamed by the children, had recently gone on an overseas trip somewhere to reward him for long service. Bad service, more like it, Danny thought sourly. And it had killed him! This was definitely something he would tell Imogen when he saw her at school tomorrow.

Making sure he was still out of earshot, Danny looked down at the note he'd stuffed into his pocket, and muttered, "Vicar, I would like to clear the air and say I'm sorry about the whole affair yesterday." He practised the whole speech. "And for you to restore your faith in me, could I help put fertilizer on your plants and pick cabbages at your allotment?" He thought he sounded silly, spouting words his dad had made him write. But still, he had to do it. Danny leaned his bicycle against the wall, and coughed to try to attract the vicar's attention away from the couple, who were now talking about their wedding.

The vicar turned round and a look of cold recognition entered his eyes when he saw him.

Danny gulped. "I would like to clear the air," he began. He could feel his face turning traffic-light red.

 Then, without warning, the horizon suddenly slipped and the sound of cackling filled Danny's ears. "I like it that your head is clear of hair…I mean, I would like to clear the air," he blurted out, desperate to correct himself.

The three adults stared at him, mouths agape.

The vicar's tone was distinctly frosty. "What is it you want to say, my son?"

Danny's mouth began working like someone who has lost control of a greasy pair of false teeth. He kept trying to force his mouth to stop uttering words he wasn't responsible for, but he finally lost the battle and began jabbering.

"Yes, I'll tell you why your head is clear of hair, even though you're sorry about the whole affair," he raved. "Once, you accidentally put hair restorer on your cabbages and the plant fertilizer on your head, and now you're as bald as an egg and have an allotment full of hairy cabbages." He finished with an evil cackle.

The old vicar's face had turned purple. "THIS IS YOUR APOLOGY?"

"Don't worry, Vicar," the hexed Danny continued heartily. "I'm sure that you can sell your hairy cabbages to this great vulture," he said, pointing at Blodwyn. "And this rock ape," nodding his head in the direction of the young man. "These scavengers look like they'd eat anything!"

The woman's face fell like a dynamited wall. "Seize the little brute, Mal!" she cried out to her partner.

A great meaty hand made a grab for Danny. Dodging out of the way, Danny ran for his bicycle and pedalled frantically away. He felt the man's fingernails rake the back of his neck as he made a desperate lunge forward on his bicycle.

Danny covered over a kilometre before he stopped pedalling. There was no sign of a pursuit. He was wheezing with exertion. No longer hexed – for now, at least – he hung his head in despair at the hopelessness of his situation. No matter how much he twisted and turned, every road led to his ruin, and his future spell behind bars drew nearer...

Meanwhile, in the present, his best trousers had been mashed into a pulp and covered in oil by his bicycle chain. When his dad heard about this latest misadventure – and saw the state of his trousers – there would be no more barbecues this century. No weekend visits from Imogen until he was in a home for the elderly. No pocket money until he was at least a hundred.

He got off his bicycle and walked up the hill towards home as slowly as a condemned man ascending the wooden steps to face the hangman and his noose.

Chapter 4

Playing the Giddy Goat

TO DANNY'S SURPRISE, when his dad saw his ragged trousers he called a doctor. Before the doctor arrived they sat in the lounge together, the atmosphere grim and silent except for the faint murmur of the television. Danny attempted to lighten the mood. "Wouldn't a seamstress or a dry-cleaner have been better?" he said with a weak smile, but immediately regretted it.

"It's not the state of your trousers I'm worried about!" Dad snapped. "That is, unless you're not wearing any in the street again. It's the state of your mind and whether you're losing it! So I've called my friend Bob Piecrust to see what he suggests."

Danny's hopes had been rising that his dad didn't know about his disastrous apology to the vicar. "I can explain…"

Mr. Cloke put up his hand to silence Danny. "Explain kicking my backside! Explain pretending to be a dog doing its business! Explain parading about in public in your underwear!" Mr. Cloke leaped to his feet and began pacing up and down the room. The decibel level was reaching that of a low-flying fighter jet. "AND EXPLAIN TELLING THE VICAR HE'S AS BALD AS AN EGG AND HAS AN ALLOTMENT FULL OF HAIRY CABBAGES!"

Danny's face turned ashen.

"Yes, just before you got back, Vicar Nannish telephoned to say that you'd given him a mouthful of cheek. I want you to go to your room and not come back down here until you stop playing the giddy goat."

Danny lay on his bed, thinking. Doctor Piecrust had just left the room, after having a friendly chat with him, asking if he was happy and if he was missing his mum terribly much. When the conversation had strayed on to his recent tomfoolery, Danny decided that mentioning the cackling Hobblegob might see him immediately carted away to a secure home behind bars, so he tried to play down the events as much as possible. But when he revisited them and mentioned kicking his dad's bottom (and the incidents involving the vicar, the lamp-post and the hairy cabbages), the doctor immediately covered his face with his hands, and great wheezing spasms had issued forth. Then he'd left the room, mumbling something about "hay fever" and that Danny had "certainly been playing the giddy goat". Danny was convinced he'd heard a roar of laughter as Doctor Piecrust went back downstairs, but he couldn't be sure.

A cool evening breeze blew gently across Danny's

face. Perhaps his situation wasn't completely hopeless though, he thought. The churchyard seemed to offer some clues as to who was behind the Zero Hex. There he had seen both S.L.A.Y.'s Malicia Clegg lurking about and the weird images of Aunt Mildred on Cyril's gravestone.

Danny decided he would sneak out the following night and return to the churchyard. He couldn't go tonight; Dad and Doctor Piecrust were now sitting in the garden, directly beneath his bedroom window – the window he planned to escape from...

Fragments of the pair's conversation drifted up to his room. "He's overwrought, Terry...first...lost...mother... now Mildred...surely it's the...been through a lot..."

"Come off it, Pie...you lost...father...hard for you... didn't kick your mother up the...and do a...on the lamp-post...or tell vicar...bald as an egg...and...hairy cabbages."

"But I...the principal...in the...and he chased me down the..."

"Shush, Pie! If Danny hears you, he might get the idea to..."

"Danny's...highly strung, that's all, Terry."

"Highly strung? He's not a poodle," Mr. Cloke said in exasperation, so loudly that Danny heard every word. "I don't know," he continued a bit more calmly, "I'm worried about him. He seems unhinged. First Mildred went off her rocker, grew a purple beard and turned into a Neanderthal woman, and now this. It's a madhouse here! If I believed in such nonsense, I would say there's a strange spell on him."

On Monday morning Danny was back at school for the first time since being cursed by the Zero Hex. Dad had dropped him off for once, because he wanted to make sure he didn't get into any more trouble. Standing beside the school gates, Danny was dreading what the hex might make him do next.

But these fears were chased away when he saw that clambering down from the bus was a girl with long red hair and pale green eyes. She waved at him.

Danny's mind floated back to when Imogen had walked into class for the first time. He remembered thinking that she was the prettiest girl he had ever seen.

That first day she'd been told by Miss Snodgrass to sit at the only free desk near the back of the room, between Danny and a tall, broad-shouldered boy with a really mean look in his eye: school bully Roger "Chopper" Chowdhury. Imogen had smiled nervously at them and gone to sit on the spare chair.

Too late, Danny had spotted the drawing pin waiting, spike upwards, on the chair and the nasty smirk on Chopper's face. Danny had felt dizzy with anger as he waited for the new girl's scream, but something very peculiar happened. Instead, it was Chopper Chowdhury howling in pain and clutching his backside. Chopper was the butt of the class jokes all day; everyone telling him he had got "a bum deal".

In the playground later that morning, Imogen had thanked Danny and said it was the best magic trick she'd ever seen. "I saw the drawing pin, you know," she added. "I was going to sweep it onto the floor at the last second and not make a fuss about it. Doesn't do to get someone into trouble on your first day. But then the pin just seemed to move of its own accord."

"It wasn't me, honestly," said Danny. "But I'm glad it happened."

"Oh, come on," scoffed Imogen, assuming Danny was being modest.

Danny continued to deny it, finally saying, "But I'll tell you who I think it was if you promise not to think I'm a loony." He had gone on to say that it was almost certainly the work of the world's most famous author, someone she would know as Cyril Spectre, who happened to be dead, and a spirit...

"What do you mean, he's a spirit?" Imogen said, goggling at Danny. "He's my hero, the writer of the best books in the world. Why on earth would he be rescuing me from a drawing pin?"

"Right at this moment, the answer to that question is

as big a mystery to me as it is to you," Danny said with a frown, then, after swearing her to secrecy, he shared all his adventures with her.

To Danny's amazement, Imogen didn't call him a liar, or a stark, staring *bonkeratic*. She looked him in the eye and said, "We both love Cyril Spectre books, and we've both been picked on by Chopper Chowdhury. It seems we have a lot in common. And I can't think for the life of me, when it seems that we might even end up being friends, why you'd make up such an incredible tale. I believe you, Danny Cloke."

Now, as Imogen hurried through the school gates, she demanded, "Whatever did you do to get the barbecue cancelled like that?" She had a breathless sort of voice that hinted at mischief and boundless enthusiasm.

"Hi, Imogen," Danny said warily, waiting for the Zero Hex to do its worst.

"Come on, spit it out," said Imogen. "You've been playing the giddy goat, Mum said."

Danny shifted uncomfortably from foot to foot. "It's all pretty unbelievable and embarrassing, you know." He leaned against the school shield framed in the middle of the gates. It read, "The Julius Rapax School – 7th Wessex".

"Ooh, just get on with it, Danny," said Imogen. "I believed you when you told me about your adventures with Cyril Spectre – and that was before I'd seen that book with you in it. If I can believe all that, I'm prepared to believe anything you tell me."

As Danny explained about his father's backside and the lamp-post and the vicar, Imogen got a fit of the giggles. "S-sorry, Danny," she said. "I know it's awful for you but – but…"

Five minutes later, as they headed to class, Imogen had finally managed to keep a straight face long enough for Danny to finish his sorry tale, including his meeting with the awful Malicia Clegg and the strange fate of Alfie Stringfellow.

Imogen looked thoughtful. "The Haloes are from the Paradise realm of Forever, right? And their enemies are the Hobblegobs of Gloom." She frowned. "And you've got a Hobblegob after you *and* a human who probably belongs to S.L.A.Y.!" she finished, getting really worked up.

"And I've got to find out who the Hobblegob and the

human are, to have any chance of beating the hex," said Danny.

"So who could have hexed you?" Imogen mused. "I think Aunt Mildred's too busy dealing with her own hex."

"Malicia Clegg's my bet," said Danny. "She seemed to know who I was in the churchyard. I reckon she's doing Aunt Mildred's dirty work."

"We can't rule out Chopper Chowdhury either," Imogen pointed out. "He's been threatening to get even with us ever since we turned three of his cheeks red during the great drawing-pin incident!" she finished with a grin.

Danny smiled back. "Or there's Miss Snodgrass! She hates me."

"She hates all of us, Danny."

"There's one other thing that puzzles me," said Danny. "How would any of these people get in contact with a Hobblegob from Gloom? It's not like making an appointment with the dentist, is it?"

"No," said Imogen thoughtfully. "So far, all the clues have been in the churchyard. I think we should go there tonight."

"Yes, that's what I'd decided," Danny said, looking at her with raised eyebrows. "But you don't have to come with me. It might be dangerous."

"You don't think I'm going to abandon you now all the fun's just beginning, do you? Anyway," she continued, looking slightly hurt, "what sort of friend would leave you alone to deal with all this?"

"I'm sorry," said Danny. "I didn't mean it like that. It's just that it said in Cyril's letter that this Zero Hex will make me act like a *disgusterous* idiot. So you'll end up hating me too." He felt a wave of hopelessness wash over him.

But Imogen was not to be beaten. "You're the only boy in the world who has ever met Cyril Spectre, so you're okay by me. You also had a copy of *A Turn in the Grave* before it even existed! I saw the year it was first printed – next year! You've shared that secret with no one else but me. So here's what I'm going to do in return. Every time you kick my backside, or turn into a dog, or burn my homework, or ask for my hand in marriage in front of large gatherings of people, I'm going to take a deep breath and say it's the Zero Hex doing it. What do you say?"

"I think I want to marry you, Imogen Falconer," said Danny.

"Ha ha!" said Imogen, then, noticing Danny's straight face, added in alarm, "That's not the hex, is it?"

Danny smiled sheepishly. "I was only joking."

"Be serious." She punched him on the arm. "So, what do you think Cyril means in his letter when he says you'll have a spell behind bars?"

"It sounds like a dark, smelly dungeon, or a lock-up for the criminally insane," Danny said glumly. They went up the steps into the school building. "But I reckon for a kid my age a spell behind bars means I'm going to end up locked in the sort of place where bad kids go."

Imogen shuddered. "Don't say that."

"Well, I can't help thinking it," said Danny. "Because it would just be the next awful thing to happen. Dad thinks I'm playing the giddy goat. My Cyril Spectre books have gone up in flames..."

"You can always borrow my copies," Imogen said as they walked along the main corridor.

"What, after I burned all mine?"

"You're right," she said hastily. "Anyway, let's keep

a careful eye on anyone else acting suspiciously."

Danny couldn't help thinking that his salvation was a long, long way off. "I wish I could have seen what happened to Aunt Mildred in her helicopter," he said with a long sigh. "I'm sure there must have been a clue there. Cyril was trying to help. I know it. But I keep missing the vital thing."

Danny and Imogen paused at their classroom door. Classmates filed past them and went inside. "You know the most important clue so far, Danny?" Her eyes shining with excitement, Imogen continued, "I think your dad's had contact with the person who placed the Zero Hex on you!"

"Oh, yeah!" Danny exclaimed. "Someone warned him about the kick up the bum. Who else could know that? But how do we get it out of Dad? Last time I asked, he nearly bit my head off."

"We'll think about it later. Right now we've got another problem. Snodgrass." Imogen reached into her school bag. "Have you done your homework?"

"No," Danny said glumly. "What with the hex thing and all, it just slipped my mind."

"I'm sure Tarquin Botfly will let you borrow the motorized pen he's just invented," said Imogen, thinking quickly. "Or his Exact Replica Parchment Copier. It's a miniature photocopying machine that fits inside an exercise book. For when you get lines – that sort of stuff."

"Mr. Cloke! Miss Falconer! Get in here at once!" a harsh voice shrieked.

Danny sighed. "The dulcet tones of Snotty Snodgrass. Compared to being behind bars, detention hardly seems like a big deal, anyway."

Imogen smiled wanly, and they took their seats near the back of the room. Their sour-faced teacher was noisily demanding everyone's homework. "Hand 'em up! Hand 'em up! There'll be Saturday morning detentions for anyone who hasn't written a minimum of ten pages. Hand up your book reviews on one of Cyril Clegg's seventeen masterpieces." Everyone groaned.

"Silence!" Miss Snodgrass had the appearance of a vicious little shrew. There were several folds of skin hanging loosely from her throat, and her hair was scraped back into a tight bun.

"Look at her," Imogen muttered out of the corner of her mouth. "She actually *wants* to give someone a detention."

"I know," Danny said bitterly. "I'm keeping her on my list of suspects."

"Detention, Chowdhury," said Miss Snodgrass. "This essay's only three words long. And two of them are your name and the other's a swear word." Then she paused before the desk of a snowy-haired boy with sticky-out ears. "Botfly, where's yours?"

"Now let me explain that it was an honest mistake," Tarquin Botfly began loftily. "One of my new inventions, the Enticing Would-You-Read-It-Twicing Boring Book Detector had been working perfectly. It's sort of like a camera, a series of flat metal plates with razor-sharp edges and the mechanical arm of a crane all put together..."

"This had better be good, Botfly," Miss Snodgrass said, tapping her foot.

Tarquin's confidence was beginning to falter. "It does a complete scan of the book in five seconds, studying front covers, plot, characters, excitement, et cetera and stores good books in its special compartment and throws boring ones to one side..."

"And?" Miss Snodgrass said dangerously.

Quickly, he handed her a plastic bag full of shredded paper.

"What's this?" she said, goggling at him.

"It went haywire, sliced up all seventeen Cyril Clegg books into tiny pieces, and then it blew up, singeing one of my eyebrows. Look," he said, lifting his fringe. "One white, one black," he finished, lamely.

Miss Snodgrass gave a gasp of horror. "You destroyed seventeen Clegg books. Four Saturday detentions for you, Botfly! And your guardian will be receiving a bill for the cost of those books, although, of course, such wonderful work is beyond price."

"Yes, Miss," Tarquin said miserably.

Little Emma Chico felt Miss Snodgrass's wrath next. "There's only half a page here," said the teacher, her eyes glittering malevolently as she read the girl's homework.

"But Clegg's books are so dull," said Emma. "Even Mum said she couldn't think of anything else to write."

Miss Snodgrass was remorseless. "Saturday morning detention for you, Miss Chico. And if your mother doesn't like it, she'd better come in and have a word with the principal about you attending a different school. We have multiple copies of all seventeen novels by Cyril Clegg in this classroom," she said, eyeing the class. "And one hundred of his 'mini readers' with set exercises. What more could you want?"

"Action," Mattie Deer said politely.

Miss Snodgrass turned to look at the skinny boy with

freckles and her voice became soft with menace. "I beg your pardon, Mr. Deer?"

"I've done my homework," Mattie added hurriedly, handing it up as she loomed in front of him. "I reviewed *The Paperclip That Didn't Do Anything Ever* and nothing happened at any stage. It doesn't even dream of doing something!"

"Horrible, childish habit, dreaming," snapped Miss Snodgrass, grabbing his homework. "Remember that, Deer and you'll go far. And another thing – next time you hand up a book review, don't write in such large letters. There are only three lines a page on here." She looked around suddenly. "Your turn, Cloke."

As Danny opened his mouth to make his excuses, a terrible cackling suddenly filled his ears. Instead of apologizing, he started giggling.

"Come on, Cloke," snapped Miss Snodgrass. "Stop grinning inanely and hand me your homework. Stop playing the giddy goat at once!"

"Giddy goat! Giddy goat!" bleated Danny. "Why is everyone saying that? Meaaaaaaaaah!" The whole class turned around and gawped at Danny.

Miss Snodgrass spluttered, "W-what? Detention, Cloke."

Danny ripped a page from his exercise book, and started to chew on it, noisily.

Imogen studied Danny's face and turned pale. "Er, let me take Danny to the sick room, Miss. He's ill…"

"Shut up, Miss Falconer!" Miss Snodgrass ordered, regaining her composure. She walked with great deliberation to her desk at the front of the classroom and placed on it the assignments she'd collected, before returning to face him. "You'd dare to play the giddy goat in my class, would you?"

"Ye-eh-eh-eh-eh-s!" said Danny. Pushing back his seat with a screech, he leaped up and frolicked and pranced down the aisles, like a goat-kid in a springtime meadow – all the while bleating loudly.

Everyone watched Danny's performance, stunned. Imogen had her head in her hands. "This is going to be harder than I thought," she muttered.

"Meaaaaaaaaah! Meaaaaaaaaah! Meaaaaaaaaah!"

Miss Snodgrass was crackling with fury. "You've got Saturday detention for a year!" This was greeted by a shocked hubbub from the rest of the class. That was an all-time punishment record. Then all eyes turned back from her to Danny.

Danny didn't seem to care. He was greedily eating the assignments on her desk – paper, staples, the lot – all the while smacking his lips and licking his fingers as if he was polishing off his favourite ice cream.

Miss Snodgrass's eyes roved around the room. "I'll be recommending that anyone laughing at these disgraceful antics will join Master Cloke on Saturday detention *and* Daily Report for the rest of the year!" she bellowed.

Despite this warning, Tarquin Botfly was the first to

snigger. And once it had escaped, the laughter was infectious. Like an all-consuming tidal wave, it swept the classroom. Miss Snodgrass advanced down the aisle towards Danny. He sized her up for a moment, then put his head down and charged like a battling billy goat. She stepped aside, alarmed, as he passed the front row of desks and tore up the aisle. He kept going straight past her, through the open classroom door and out into the corridor. A ragged cheer went up.

Miss Snodgrass chased Danny along the corridor. "I'm taking you to the principal!" she yelled after him.

But the goat boy could smell the open air, the fields and the wild call of the mountaintops, and he easily outdistanced her, bounding through a door as he clicked his heels together, then across the playground and out into the streets beyond. "Meaaaaaaaaah! Meaaaaaaaaah! Meaaaaaaaaah!" he bleated loudly all the way, Miss Snodgrass's outraged shrieks getting fainter and fainter behind him.

Danny was halfway home when the hex released him. Shocked to find himself in someone's front garden with a mouthful of marigolds, Danny looked around him at the devastation he'd caused. The flowerbeds had been trampled, the roses were half chewed and great tufts taken out of the lawn. An irate woman was banging on the window and gesticulating wildly at him. In the other hand she held a telephone to her ear, and Danny watched her clearly mouth the word "Police".

Gathering his wits, Danny groaned, "Oh, no," spraying little bits of yellow petal in all directions in the process. He sped off, guessing that the police were already on their way, hoping the woman hadn't recognized him and wasn't going to report him to his dad. How could he bear the look of disappointment in his dad's eyes again? But policemen were worse. Policemen handed you over to judges who handed out spells behind bars…

Danny considered running away from home and becoming a pirate. In the end, he decided to go to the churchyard while he still had the chance. Dad would never let him out of his sight after this latest performance and he just had to see if there were any more clues about the Zero Hex at Cyril's gravestone. It was his only hope.

Chapter 5

The Warning

BENEATH A SLATE-GREY SKY, Danny hurried across the churchyard towards the holly bush in the middle. Glancing around furtively, he was relieved to see that the place was deserted.

With a last nervous look over his shoulder, Danny stepped in front of Cyril's gravestone. He reached out and touched the cold marble. Immediately, the gravestone swirled and revealed within its strange depths the celestial television screen. Danny felt a surge of relief.

The images were the same as before: Aunt Mildred and Mr. Lopez in the helicopter; then the world leader of S.L.A.Y., Julius Rapax, appearing, grainy-looking, on the videophone. Danny watched impatiently, until finally it got to the part he hadn't seen.

As Danny continued to watch, Rapax – a tiny figure within the helicopter's videophone – put up a hand to silence Aunt Mildred. "Calm yourself, my dear. It is true that we're dealing with the spirit realm here and that is always tricky." There was the merest foreign lilt to Rapax's voice. "When you have as much money as I do, you can find out *anything*. And you're quite right. It has been confirmed that your tormentor was indeed Cyril Spectre, known in life as Cyril Clegg."

"Cyril Spectre? This is all beginning to make sense," Aunt Mildred said, ponderingly.

Rapax continued. "Anyway, in order to defeat a magic spell known as the Hero Hex and enter Paradise, Cyril *Spectre* – as he then became – needed the help of a human child. And this turned out to be your stepson, Danny Cloke. As payment for Master Cloke's assistance, Cyril inflicted these hexes upon you."

Aunt Mildred's face took on a venomous expression. "All this happened to me because of Danny and that stupid author of his? I don't care what it takes, Julius. That child will suffer undreamed-of misery for this." Looking on, Danny had a horrible, creeping feeling all the way down his spine.

"Your situation isn't so bad," Rapax continued mildly. "You have nothing more than a rather nasty combination of minor hexes – child's play, really."

"Minor!" roared Aunt Mildred.

Rapax seemed to be studying Aunt Mildred closely. He went on, "During the past few weeks my spies have discovered quite a lot about the hexes inflicted upon you. Ultimately, what we have learned is that, as things stand, one of the many scavenging animals you have crazed with your odour will finally eat you. That is your ultimate fate if Cyril's hexes are not countered. This will happen before 12.07 tomorrow afternoon (GMT)."

Aunt Mildred's eyes bulged.

"As you know, at the time you were cursed, you were carrying out an important task for me – a task that you have been working on for four and a half years. But if you die tomorrow, you will not be able to complete it and this will be most inconvenient for me."

"And for *me*," said Aunt Mildred pointedly.

"Indeed. It is my wish that you also continue S.L.A.Y.'s mission to enslave every child in the world," lisped Julius Rapax. "But, of course, it's a problem that you are still hexed. And so we must get you unhexed. To do that you must meet your dearly departed grandfather, the deliciously wicked Neville Neville. He's a spirit nowadays, a type known as a Hobblegob. He has taken to calling himself Cat O' Nine Tails. Anyway, you're to meet him at his gravestone in the Under-the-Sod Cemetery at midnight tonight. If you summon him, I think Neville Neville will be prepared to counter the curses placed on you. As it happens, he seems to hate Danny too, although I haven't been able to find out why."

"Thank you for your help, Julius," said Aunt Mildred, her eyes gleaming. The image on the videophone flickered and Julius Rapax was gone.

Helicopter pilot Lopez glanced over at Aunt Mildred, a terrified look on his face. "What's all that about hexes and meeting your dead grandfather…?"

"None of your business," Aunt Mildred snapped nastily. "Leave the spooky stuff to me. You just fly the chopper."

"But Mildred," Lopez insisted, his face as pale as if he'd seen a Hobblegob already. "Aren't we meddling with things we don't understand? We'd…"

"WATCH OUT, LOPEZ!" cried Aunt Mildred. "You're going to crash!" They veered away from the mountainside, where a lone wolf stood greedily watching them, enraptured by Aunt Mildred's odour.

Abruptly, Cyril's gravestone became merely that once more. Danny sat on a grassy mound to think about what he'd just seen. His mind was racing. When had all this happened? Had Aunt Mildred had her meeting? Did this mean that she was the human who'd put the Zero Hex on Danny? Was Neville Neville the Hobblegob who'd helped her? Danny had no proof. But it might be worth investigating Neville Neville's gravestone. If Cyril's gravestone held special properties, then Aunt Mildred's grandfather's might too. He wondered briefly what possible reason Neville Neville could have for hating him. Was it because Danny was the enemy of Aunt Mildred, perhaps?

He stood up and started looking around for Neville Neville's grave.

As he scanned the headstones for the name, Danny caught sight of a hunched figure walking down the road alongside the churchyard: Malicia Clegg! She was peering over the hedge.

Was she spying again? She certainly didn't seem to be here to mourn her late husband, Danny thought, judging by the way that she was stalking about, as if searching for something – or *someone*.

Suddenly, Malicia looked in Danny's direction. He crouched down behind Cyril's gravestone, and leaned his head against the smooth marble, breathing very fast. For a second it felt as though his head passed through the solid stone. He glanced at it in surprise. And got quite a start when he saw Cyril looking right back at him, from within the headstone itself.

He wasn't quite the same as Danny remembered him.

The deep wrinkles on his face had smoothed out and his hair and beard were not quite as wild. He was still as ghostly and translucent as before, and he appeared to be floating. The old-fashioned three-piece suit he wore was a dazzling white, like the light of the sun woven into cloth. Attached by a chain to the waistcoat pocket was his fob watch, but instead of hands and numbers on it, displayed on the face was a single "1" in its centre, revolving slowly.

"Cyril!" Danny said with a delighted grin.

"*Respectrely* at your service once again, Master Cloke," said Cyril in a voice that was like the moaning of the wind around the gravestones.

"Am I glad to see you," said Danny. "Can you help me? Do you know what's going on?"

"I've been *mordained* to *happy-peer* before you," said Cyril. "But although I can speak to you, I cannot use my *magnifantabulous hexcellence* to rescue you. You have to defeat the Hobble—" Without warning, there was a haze of static and Cyril's image was lost.

"Cyril, come back!" cried Danny in exasperation. "Are Aunt Mildred and Neville Neville responsible for the hex? And what does a spell behind bars mean?"

The image faded back into view. "...the S.A.I.N.T.s hoped that the images of Aunt Mildred and her *telechopter* would help you. Especially after my letter to you was *tampercepted*. I'm further away from you than the most distant star, so the slight time delay means this conversation is also open to *tampstering* from those *scumbletons* the Hobblegobs. Now listen closely. There is something you must protect...close to your heart..." The picture flickered again, and Cyril disappeared.

Danny groaned. What about the spell behind bars? And how was he supposed to break the Zero Hex? That was what he needed to know. It looked as though someone was interfering with Cyril's message again, just as they had done with his letter. And Cyril had been about to tell him something important. But what?

"...the Hobblegob Neville Neville is responsible," said Cyril, reappearing on the gravestone, blissfully unaware that someone was playing tricks with his transmission. "This Hobblegob has forged a *ghoulsome* pen which can be used to capture evil magic, and cast hexes and jinxes. It's called a hex pen. But because spirits are not meant to interfere in the mortal world, it needs a human to actually bring the curse into being by composing the letter and writing it in a special way. If you find the human's lett…you'll know…"

Cyril's transmission was fading once again. Then Danny heard a high-pitched screech. Looking around, he saw something extraordinary happening to a nearby headstone. It seemed to be pulsing, and a dark aura was emanating from the stone. As he watched, fascinated, Danny saw thousands of black, glistening dots within it – like flecks of oil with the colours of the rainbow inside – growing larger, forming together into the shape of a Hobblegob. The evil apparition mesmerized Danny. It was terrifying.

It floated out of its gravestone, and soared up into the sky, ready to go about its wicked schemes.

"Danny," Cyril's voice cut in abruptly. "I've replaced the patch, but I can do no more. Goodbye, friend." And with these final words, his voice was cut off. Cyril had gone. Malicia Clegg was nowhere to be seen. Danny was left confused and alone in the cemetery. He walked tentatively over to the forbidding black headstone that just moments before had been seething with evil. As he got closer, he could make out the jagged lettering carved into the rock:

Neville Neville.

Chapter 6

Grounded and Floored

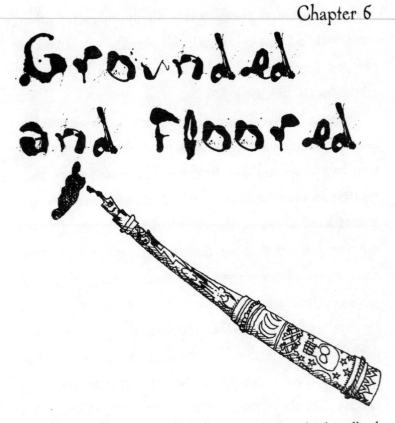

BY THE END of the school day Danny had walked back to the gates to wait for Imogen. As he watched the children stream out of the school building, he suddenly remembered where he'd seen Mr. Lopez before. Dad had pointed him out a couple of weeks ago when they were having lunch at the local hotel, The Six Gold

Stars. Apparently, Lopez was a shady character who'd been locked up in prison cells all over the world and for the past few months had been living in the hotel, much to the locals' disgust.

Imogen arrived, breathless with questions. They walked home together and Danny told her everything that had happened. By the time they parted ways, they had come up with a plan. It was decided that Imogen would hang about at The Six Gold Stars Hotel, to listen out for any clues about Lopez. And in the meantime Danny would search his own house. Somewhere, he guessed, there was a letter written with an evil hex pen. Perhaps the warning to Dad about receiving a kick up the backside was contained in the hex letter, too? If they could lay their hands on it, then they would know for certain that they were dealing with Aunt Mildred and Neville Neville the Hobblegob. Only then could they begin to think of ways to break the Zero Hex. But before Danny could start his investigations, he had to face his father once more...

As he stepped inside the house, Danny realized with a jolt that his dad was already home. Through the open living-room door, Danny could see him sitting in his chair, brooding in front of a blank television screen. He wasn't normally home at this time. Since Aunt Mildred's departure, a family friend, Mrs. Boatswain, normally came to look after Danny in the two hours before Dad came home from work. As his dad turned to look round at him, shame and sadness utterly consumed Danny. The laughter they'd shared at the funfair and at the movies and the zoo seemed like it belonged to a different lifetime. He could see from the expression in his eyes that Dad already knew about the goat business at school.

And yet, little more than two days ago they'd been laughing in the garden together.

"Sit down, Danny," Dad intoned, and Danny knew he was in for a lecture. Dad began by saying that Danny appeared to have been playing up deliberately to spite him. After hushing Danny's protests, he went on to explain that the school had telephoned to say they were putting Danny on Daily Report for the rest of the school year. "What it means," Mr. Cloke warned him, "is that at the end of each day the teachers and the principal will decide whether your behaviour is deserving of a tick or a cross. Two more crosses and they will recommend having you transferred to a school for badly behaved children."

Danny's blood ran cold at these words.

"Oh, and by the way, Danny, I'm grounding you for a year. You'll spend every evening in your bedroom, considering your actions. And to think that earlier today I was really happy for you that there's a surprise waiting upstairs."

By now, Danny felt so defeated, that the single, faint ray of hope at the end of Dad's speech didn't even register in his brain. He was so desperate for his dad not to be angry with him, and to break the power of the Zero Hex, that he was willing to try anything; even telling the truth. Grown-ups were always going on about how honesty was the best policy. He could at least give it a try.

"Dad, you were right," Danny said with a sigh. "I'm not unhinged. There *is* a strange spell on me. Please listen to my side of the story," he pleaded, seeing the look forming on his dad's face.

"I'm listening," Dad said tiredly.

"It all started with the Cyril Spectre books. I know it's going to be hard for you to believe, but…"

Danny attempted an explanation about the writer who turned out to be a Spectre, the book spirited from a year in the future, the vanishing golden envelope and magic ink. Dad listened in stony silence.

As Danny got to the part about "Zero Hexes that make you act in *disgusterous* ways" and that he believed it was "a child-hating society's wicked plot", he saw his dad's lips narrow. He trailed off weakly with, "Imogen has seen some of the magic too. Well, a tiny bit of it…"

His patience now exhausted, Dad said, "And which tiny bit would that be, Danny? The quick glimpse of Paradise, perhaps? Or her favourite author haunting her house? No, I've got it! She's having a weekend display of her favourite invisible envelopes!"

"Please, Dad, you've got to believe me," said Danny. "Imogen's seen the book from the future. It was called *A Turn in the Grave*. Unfortunately I…er, burned it when I was being hexed…but…"

Dad held up his hand for silence. "These lies are only doubling the trouble, son. But they've done something else too." With these cryptic words hanging in the air, he ordered Danny to his room with no dinner.

As Danny stumped upstairs he heard his dad pick up the phone in the hall…

Although Danny could see why his dad was so angry, there seemed to be something more to it. The mocking way Dad had dismissed his explanation (however implausible), sending him to his room with no dinner and grounding him for a year – *a year!* – was just too extreme. His dad had always been a sympathetic man, and in the past had even given Danny little hints that he and Doctor Piecrust had been "a pair of rascals" when they were boys. But now Dad just didn't want to know. Had he been hexed as well?

As soon as Danny entered his room he saw three letters from his mother waiting on the bed. He realized that this was the surprise waiting for him.

The last letter Danny had received from his mother was postmarked February 6th. It had arrived some time after Aunt Mildred's humiliating retreat from the house. Now here were three more, the date they were written printed in her handwriting in the bottom left-hand corner of each envelope: February 13th, February 27th, and March 20th.

Danny read them in order, lingering over every word and reading each of the long letters several times before finally moving on to the next one. At first his mother's tales were filled with great hope and grand adventure. She had discovered a jungle waterfall that fell so far that it seemed to reach into forever. She'd had a narrow escape from a shoal of savage piranhas and been befriended by a toucan.

The constant thread through all these escapades was always her search for the fabulously rare bird, the Long-tailed Pink Polka-dotted Home-wrecking Cuckoo; just a flick of its wings away from being captured and immortalized by Mum's camera.

But as Danny read on, the shadow of something wicked and dangerous started to creep across the pages. It was barely perceptible at first, but Danny's forehead was deeply etched with a frown by the time he opened the final envelope. His frown didn't entirely disappear even when he found a Polaroid shot of the most magnificent bird he'd ever seen soaring through the air – a wonderful creature with a haughty, almost royal demeanour and a tail like a cloud of cherry blossom.

Danny read the last letter with mounting trepidation:

ATTENTION: Danny Cloke

45 Sting Close
Nettle Bottom
Wessex
WX1 0UCH

March 20th

Dear Danny,

I have found the Long-tailed Pink Polka-dotted Home-wrecking Cuckoo! Yes, found it and photographed it, darling Danny. Years of work complete. To see it for the very first time, its plumage in flight as beautiful as the last pink clouds of sunset…oh, the beauty of that sight is almost beyond words. I was lucky enough to have my camera ready in the instant that it spread out its majestic wings just above me. As the camera shutter clicked, a lance of sunlight cut through the lush foliage and shone upon the magical bird, infusing its feathers with a glorious burnished pink. As it flew into the distance it began to utter its magnificent song, a rapid series of liquid notes of amazing variety. It was only then that I realized that tears were falling down my cheeks. They were tears of happiness.

I know I should feel that happiness still, as I write you these words, and yet…and yet…

First we found numerous feathers belonging to the bird scattered along a particular stretch of the coast. After questioning the locals there, my guide, Diego, suggested a boat trip across to a tiny desert island called Bella Vista.

And that's where we found it. I was going to make copies of this photograph (enclosed) to grace the front covers of magazines and newspapers all over the world. But now I think it's better to wait until these birds are once more safe from harm. It is better that their existence and their whereabouts are kept secret for now. So this photograph is very

precious, Danny. It's the only print currently in existence. But I wanted to share it with you, my dear son, the beauty and joy of this wondrous creature.

Danny slid the photograph into the top left-hand pocket of his jacket, and continued reading.

Soon after that first sighting, acting on a tip-off, Diego and I crept through the jungle and eavesdropped on a night-time campfire conversation. We soon realized we had a band of poachers on our trail. At first I had no idea who they were, only that they wanted to capture the cuckoo and sell it. Can you imagine my shock when I heard them say they've been on my trail for years? I must stop them somehow, or it'll be the end of this majestic bird. Keep this photograph safe, Danny. It's very important.

And the worst of it is that I know who these people are. If only I hadn't been so stupid. I want to put things right. So I must go to Sta

At that moment, the page was snatched from him with such force that all he was left with were two tiny scraps of blue paper. But for Danny, the very worst moment since the Zero Hex began was when he looked up. His heart lurched.

He was staring straight into Aunt Mildred's ugly face. The bald, purple-bearded ape-woman with the sloping forehead was gone.

"You're back!" Danny croaked.

"Did you ever doubt it?" Aunt Mildred smiled her horrible, lipless grimace. "Your father called me earlier and told me all about your disgraceful behaviour. Naturally I raced round here to be by his side. And you don't deserve these," she said, snatching up the rest of Danny's letters from the bed and pocketing them. Then, with an evil grin, she added, "What, no kiss for your wicked stepmother?" puckering up her revolting, vulture-like face; her ridiculous hair, heaped up like candyfloss, was waving from side to side.

"I'd rather kiss Cuddles," said Danny, who'd turned very pale.

Aunt Mildred was about to retaliate when they heard Dad's voice calling from downstairs. "Honeybunch," he said in such a simpering voice that it made Danny's blood boil, "I've unpacked your slippers. And there's a cup of tea down here for you."

Why was Dad being such a creep? Danny thought savagely. It was pathetic that he'd let Aunt Mildred back so easily. Perhaps he was under a spell too.

"I'm coming, darling," Aunt Mildred called back in her sweetest voice. Then her tone changed as she hissed at Danny, "You look thin. Your father tells me he sent you up here with no dinner. Call me an old softie, but I insist on making you something."

Danny remained slumped on his bed as Aunt Mildred continued. "Hmmm – now what's it to be? Spaghetti and housefly meatballs? A poisonous puffer fish in batter? Squashed hedgehog pie? A snake's egg omelette, perhaps? No, I've got it! Tonight's speciality of the house will be fried hair from the plughole, to be followed by horse-manure ice cream with sprinkles of dandruff. And in case you're thinking of snooping about anywhere tonight, you'll find an old friend has the run of the house." She marched out and slammed the door triumphantly.

But before the door closed Danny had caught a quick glimpse of dirty yellow fur with blackish spots and a curled-up, lank black tail behind her: Cuddles, the laughing hyena, was back too.

At that moment Danny realized that everything Cyril Spectre had done to get rid of Aunt Mildred had been in vain. His wicked stepmother was back. Only this time it was far, far worse. Danny himself was hexed. And Cyril Spectre couldn't save him.

Chapter 7

Dead Trouble

THE NEXT MORNING all the pupils and teachers at Danny's school gathered in the great hall for the weekly assembly. There was a general hubbub while everyone waited for the principal to arrive. Danny and Imogen sat with the rest of Class 6LP near the back of the auditorium.

Danny was telling Imogen about his disastrous evening. "I couldn't even check Dad's study for the hex letter. Cuddles slept right outside my door all night." Danny smiled half-heartedly. "At least it gobbled up Aunt Mildred's disgusting meal when I threw it at it."

"Hey, Danny." It was Chopper Chowdhury. "I don't want to *get your goat up*, but you sure acted like a *kid* yesterday!" The rest of the row sniggered.

"I'd be careful if I were you," said one of Chopper's gang, the boulder-headed Vinnie Krakouer, joining in, "or you'll be made into a *scapegoat*."

"Ignore them," Imogen whispered, as Danny struggled to fit the cuckoo photograph he'd been showing her back into the inside pocket of his jacket. "Anyway, I've got something important to tell you."

At that moment the principal began climbing the wooden steps to the stage and the auditorium fell silent. Imogen leaned right over and mumured into Danny's ear. "Apparently, your Aunt Mildred's been staying at The Six Gold Stars since last Wednesday. The staff are still gossiping about the fact that before that, a purple-bearded ape-woman had a suite there…"

From the end of their row, Miss Snodgrass shushed Imogen.

Danny thought about this. Aunt Mildred had probably arrived at The Six Gold Stars with her purple beard some time ago, perhaps even when she'd first fled their house. But she'd only turned up at the hotel looking normal – well, normal for her – last Wednesday. So Neville Neville must've taken the hex off her. Had they decided to Zero Hex Danny at the same time? By Saturday, Danny had been Zero Hexed. And last night, Aunt Mildred had turned up at their house less than half an hour after Dad had made that telephone call. It was almost as if she'd been waiting to be called back...

As Principal Peregrine Strauss strode across the stage, Danny studied him with distaste. He was a squat man who dressed outrageously. Today he wore a cream-coloured cricket blazer and a Turkish fez perched on top of his head. He stood in the middle of the platform, arms behind his back, eyes scanning the sea of faces. There was something creepy and menacing about him.

Mr. Strauss stepped behind the podium and fiddled with the microphone. It let out a sudden squeal of

feedback and everyone put their hands to their ears. "Ladies and gentlemen," he said in a hissing voice that reminded Danny of a snake, "and boys and girls of Julius Rapax School, down to business..."

Danny remembered the connection between the name of his school and S.L.A.Y.'s world leader. What could it mean?

"I have a couple of sundry items to get through," the principal continued. "Firstly, starting next term, Neville & Neville Caterers will be running the tuck shop..."

"That's one of Aunt Mildred's companies!" Danny whispered to Imogen. "Neville Neville and Neville Neville Junior are her grandfather and father."

The principal went on remorselessly. "…the playing of hand tennis on the flagstones in the playground is banned forthwith." A groan sounded around the hall. "It's now on the 'Outlawed' list, together with football, cricket and the use of skipping ropes." Principal Strauss shouted over the noise, "Might I suggest that for those of you seeking entertainment of the sporting variety, you should make your way to the Clegg Memorial Playground behind the temporary toilets and play his justifiably famous bead-clicking game on the apparatus provided." There were mutinous mutterings all around the auditorium.

Ignoring them, Peregrine Strauss went on, "Now to the main topic of today's assembly. I have a very important announcement! As some of you are no doubt aware, Alfie Stringfellow, the school caretaker, has sadly died." The children let out gasps, mainly of shock, but mixed with relief.

"Alfie Stringfellow will be sorely missed," said Mr. Strauss. "He was a familiar face around the school, and for many of us, a friend. On a personal note, Alfie and I even belonged to the same club... Ahem, anyway, he had recently flown overseas and the tragedy happened while he was there."

"Stringfellow was a horrid man," Imogen whispered to Danny.

"He was in S.L.A.Y., for sure," Danny added in the same undertone.

"Imogen Falconer! Danny Cloke!" Mr. Strauss hissed suddenly. "Come and join me on stage and share your whispered conversation with the rest of the school. Now!"

"Oh, meaaaaaaaaaah-vellous," Chopper bleated softly, sneering at them as they passed. "Cloke and Falconer are finally for the hi-i-i-i-i-gh jump."

Danny could feel every pair of eyes in the school upon them as they trudged slowly to the front of the hall.

"Repeat your conversation into the microphone," said Mr. Strauss.

"We...we were discussing how we felt about Mr. Stringfellow's, er, passing," Imogen said in a weak little voice.

As Danny stepped up to the microphone, the world suddenly tilted, and he staggered like a drunken sailor on the high seas.

A few children in the front rows sniggered.

"Your turn, Mr. Cloke. Speak into the microphone," said Mr. Strauss coldly. "Tell the school how you feel about Mr. Stringfellow's passing."

"It's better than him failing," Danny said, his ears filled with the cackling of the Hobblegob. His face twisting with effort, he continued, "String Bean will be sorely missed. How can we forget all those bouts of pneumonia after he turned the sprinklers on us during school sports day? Or all those wonderful bites on our bodies after he put fleas in the coconut matting? He was – he...hee hee hee hee hee hee," Danny giggled without warning. He struggled to control himself. The audience looked on, mouths hanging open.

"Although he *slayed* us a hundred times, we don't harbour a grudge, do we, school? We don't harbour a – har –, hah! Hah! Hah! Hah! Hah! Hah! Hah! Hah! Hah! Hah!" He lost all control, roaring and whooping with laughter.

Before Danny even knew what was happening, Mr. Strauss had grabbed him and dragged him offstage towards his office. The assembly finished in disarray. Imogen stood alone on stage for a moment, and then decided to follow Danny and Principal Strauss.

"What did you follow me for? You'll only get in trouble too," Danny hissed as Imogen joined him just inside the door of the school secretary's office. Principal Strauss was behind his desk in the next room, having an animated telephone conversation.

Imogen shrugged. "Just trying to look after you, I suppose. When the principal gets off the phone," she said, trying to look confident, "I'm going to tell him you've been stung by a starfish and the poison's made you go funny in the head."

"Can you be stung by a starfish? Anyway, he's not going to fall for that," said Danny. "Listen. Just as Strauss was about to lose his rag with me, his receptionist 'bleeped' him to say my dad's widget factory was on the phone returning his call. I was panicking, of course, but the call's not about me at all. Strauss sends his secretary off on some errand, and then places a huge order for widgets. Says he'll be doing the ordering himself from now on, instead of Alfie Stringfellow."

"What's going on?" said Imogen. "Is it something to do with S.L.A.Y.? The more we find out, the less I understand it."

"Look, you'd better get out of here," said Danny. "You might end up being grounded or doing loads of detentions, and then you won't be able to help me beat the Zero Hex."

"Mmm, okay," said Imogen, looking doubtful. "Good luck." She smiled and hurried away.

A moment later, Principal Strauss put down the telephone. He called Danny back into his office, and studied him with a beady eye. "I see your last friend in the world's just deserted you, Cloke."

"Yes, sir."

"Hand me your Daily Report book." A gnarled hand attached to a long bony arm shot across the desk.

Danny removed the little red book from his pocket. The photograph of the Long-tailed Pink Polka-dotted

Home-wrecking Cuckoo had got wedged inside it. He removed it hurriedly and handed Principal Strauss the book, shoving the photograph back in his pocket. "What was that?" the principal demanded.

"Just a photograph of Tarquin Botfly's talking Irish wolfhound, sir," Danny lied.

"Now, there's a boy with talent," said the principal, leaning back in his swivel chair and gazing into space. "Talent that needs to be harnessed. Now, where was I? Oh, yes." He opened Danny's book at today's date and, with a thick black pen, drew a cross the size of the entire page.

Just one more could mean a bad boys' school for Danny. And there was still the rest of the week to go – and a whole term after that. "Sir, I would like to try and explain—" Danny began.

"When you indulged yourself in that disgraceful performance on stage," said Principal Strauss, cutting across Danny's speech and fixing him with his most piercing stare, "why did you say that Alfie Stringfellow '*slayed* you a hundred times'?"

Danny wondered why Principal Strauss was so

interested. Had Danny given himself away? Who, after all, but a member of S.L.A.Y. would ask such a strange question, about a single word? "It's – it's just a thing that kids say, Principal. An expression, that's all," he said, trying to assume his best innocent look.

"GET OUT!" yelled Principal Strauss so abruptly that Danny's chair legs screeched across the floor as he jumped backwards. He scrambled up and scuttled outside, his ears still ringing.

Danny was surprised to see Aunt Mildred advancing across the playground towards the principal's office. "What's she doing here?" he muttered to himself. She had shown absolutely no interest in Danny's schooling over the years, and as far as he knew, this was her first visit.

Danny ducked behind a wall. He smelled a strong whiff of perfume mixed with *eau de hyena* as Aunt Mildred strode by. Peeping out from his hiding place, Danny saw her step into the outer office. The principal came out and shook hands with her. Then he showed her into his inner office. The door closed.

His heart hammering somewhere near his throat,

Danny crept round the corner and crouched below the window of the principal's office.

"Awful business, Alfie's, eh?" Danny heard the principal say.

"Casualties of war!" said Aunt Mildred. "Saw it with my own eyes. Nasty. Could have been me. Anyway, there's no time to be squeamish. I've already found a replacement. The hotel manager at The Six Gold Stars is keen to join. Smurthwaite, his name is. I told him there's an overseas trip coming up."

"Have you got any idea when yet, Mildred?"

"No. But once I find it we'll have to leave almost immediately. I'll tell you all about it at the extraordinary general meeting on Friday..." Then her voice was gone.

Cursing that he couldn't hear more of this curious conversation, Danny wondered how their voices had been cut off suddenly. He had to know more.

Hearing nothing, he stole out from his hiding place, crept round the corner, slowly opened the door into the outer office, then crossed it and turned the doorknob to the principal's room. The door creaked. He froze. There was still no sound. He peered inside. Seeing nothing, he pushed the door open fractionally wider...

Aunt Mildred and Principal Strauss had gone. In a room with only one door and a window they couldn't possibly have climbed through, because he'd been crouched beneath it, they had vanished into thin air.

Chapter 8

The Hex Letter

THE HOURS AND DAYS in Danny's life limped by like wounded animals, until finally it was Friday night.

Danny was lying on his bed, staring at the ceiling. He wondered bleakly how many more days of freedom he had. This time last week Dad had suggested having the barbecue and Danny had excitedly rung Imogen to invite her and her mum for lunch. How long ago that seemed now. He and Imogen had arranged a rendezvous in the garden later to discuss their latest findings, but they didn't seem to be making much progress towards stopping the Zero Hex or finding out more about S.L.A.Y. He looked down at the watery soup that Aunt Mildred had made him take upstairs for dinner. It had bits of raw cabbage and dead mosquitoes floating in it.

Being trapped in the house with Aunt Mildred again was worse than ever before. She had filled his room with books – a hundred and seventeen of them to be precise – the seventeen Cyril Clegg novels and one hundred mini readers with set exercises. Dad was hardly ever at home; he seemed to be working all hours at the widget factory, and Aunt Mildred came and went as she pleased. "I'll *baby*sit while you're so busy," she'd said to Danny's dad, adding, "This is the biggest widget order you've ever had, Terry. You don't want to mess it up." And to Danny's horror and disgust, Dad had agreed to her offer. Danny couldn't believe his dad would be capable of such treachery after everything he knew she'd done to his son. It *must* be a spell affecting him, Danny thought, desperately hoping that was the case.

Danny watched the shadows creep across his room until it was in darkness. A bright full moon shone through his window, and he was still pondering. The conversation he'd overheard between the principal and Aunt Mildred seemed to confirm that Principal Strauss was involved in S.L.A.Y. How had they managed to disappear like that? There had to be some sort of secret exit from the principal's office, but he couldn't risk being caught looking for it, not with only one cross to go in his report book. And there was something decidedly peculiar about Alfie Stringfellow's death. Aunt Mildred had been there too. And what possible reason could the school principal have for placing a huge order for his dad's widgets? Did Aunt Mildred have a hand in that too?

And the number of locals involved in S.L.A.Y. was taking on frightening proportions: Aunt Mildred and the late Alfie Stringfellow. Principal Strauss – almost certainly. Miss Snodgrass, probably. Malicia Clegg. The helicopter pilot, Lopez.

Imogen had discovered nothing more at The Six Gold Stars. The only thing Danny could be thankful for was that he'd made it through to the end of the week without the dreaded third cross in his Daily Report book.

On Wednesday he should have received the final cross. The hex had struck again. He'd thrown a steak and kidney pie into Chopper Chowdhury's face while he stood in the canteen queue, but Imogen took the blame for it and received a detention for her troubles.

Then yesterday morning, at Imogen's prompting, Danny had thanked Chopper for not telling the principal that he had thrown the pie.

"If you hadn't given us all such a good laugh in assembly yesterday, I would've done," Chopper said, with a hint of admiration. "If you keep up the good work I might let you join my gang."

"Who wants to be in a gang led by a flea-bitten baboon!" replied a suddenly hexed Danny. He had spent break-times for the rest of the day on the run, hiding in storerooms, cupboards and bins to avoid Chopper, before being chased all the way home after school.

Danny turned his mind to the present. Once he'd

summoned up enough courage, he planned to sneak into the study to begin searching for the hex letter he was sure his dad had been sent. Unusually, Cuddles wasn't around; Aunt Mildred had muttered something about the vet's. Anyhow, this might be his only chance.

On the pretext of visiting the bathroom, Danny checked to see what Aunt Mildred was doing. Peering downstairs, he saw her vulture-like neck stooping over the hallway's telephone as she spoke into it.

Danny crept along the landing, one step and then a pause, another step and a pause, so that the floorboards wouldn't creak and give him away. With each step he listened out for any signs of movement downstairs. The sound of his heart thumping in his chest was so loud he was afraid that it would give him away.

Finally, he reached his dad's study. It was an impressive room with a big picture window. It was dominated by an antique desk with an expensive computer and ornate globe on it. Danny rummaged with shaking hands through the papers on the desk. But they were just a bunch of bills, junk mail and office reports. The bin contained similar items, only screwed up, and coated in the remains of a mushy, overripe banana.

Wiping his hands on the back of his jeans, Danny tried the top drawer of the desk. It was locked. Exasperated, he whirled the ball of the globe around. It made a clunking, rattling sound. Danny panicked, thinking Aunt Mildred would hear the noise. In his haste to stop the globe spinning, he knocked it over.

It teetered for a moment...

...and finally came to rest safely in Danny's arms. He gently replaced it on the desk, his heart hammering wildly.

The globe was still spinning slightly. There was an odd, metallic *swooosh swooosh swooosh* coming from it, a softer sound this time. There was something inside the globe. He prised the ball apart at the line of the Equator. Inside were a pressed flower, a dead spider – and a small brass key.

Danny grabbed the key and tried it in the top drawer of the desk. It was a perfect fit. He turned the key and opened it. Empty. Disappointed, he tried the second drawer. Inside were two photographs, one of Danny when he was about five, standing between his mum and dad, and another, of Danny's mum when she was no more than eighteen. He felt hot tears prick his eyes. His mother had the kindest smile he'd ever seen. He wanted to keep the photographs, but reluctantly locked the drawer again, leaving them inside.

Hands shaking slightly, Danny opened the last drawer. His heart gave a little jump.

There in front of him was an envelope addressed to his dad. Danny recognized Aunt Mildred's handwriting immediately.

He picked it up and took out the letter. It was handwritten too. He began to read it, his face slowly turning the colour of porridge.

The Six Gold Stars Hotel, Turnips Lane, Upon-the-Sod, Wessex WX1 0YYY

Terry Cloke
45 Sting Close
Nettle Bottom
Wessex
WX1 0UCH

Friday, April 18th

Dear Terry,

I've left this letter until now because I thought I'd let the dust settle. I know you think I'm a monster. Frankly I don't blame you. But I would like to explain a few things from my point of view. I know you were appalled when the police arrested me and I called the police sergeant "a horse's bum". I know you were disgusted when my hair turned purple, then fell out and grew back on my face. It was disgraceful that I suddenly smelled like I'd been sleeping in a ditch for a month, and was finally chased out of the neighbourhood by my own darling pet, which had been crazed by my rank smell.

I'm sorry to tell you this next bit because it will hurt you, but the doctors say that it all happened because I had a nervous reaction to <u>Danny</u>'s behaviour.

I did my best to love the boy but it rebounded back on me like he was <u>throwing pies</u> in my face. Whenever you weren't around he just ran wild, always <u>playing</u> <u>the giddy goat,</u> <u>shouting out things in public,</u> <u>laughing at inappropriate times</u> and <u>dishing out</u> <u>insults.</u> <u>Terry...you must believe me about this.</u>

I'm sorry I fed <u>Danny</u> food from the hyena's bowl on one occasion. That was only because one evening I reached into the fridge to get his smoked salmon supper and as I bent down he gave me several <u>kicks up</u> <u>the bottom.</u> It's true that I forced him to sit in the broom cupboard at my fashion shop too. That was because he kept <u>cocking his leg like a dog</u> every time customers came into the shop.

I didn't want you to worry about all this, knowing how hard you work. And by the time you got home, <u>Danny</u> was always in bed, <u>burning</u> the midnight oil, reading <u>Cyril Spectre books,</u> not bothering to wait up for you. So you didn't see the worst of his behaviour.

Mark my words: <u>it will all end for Danny with a</u> <u>spell behind bars. And the moment he's alone behind</u> <u>bars, he'll be lost to a life of crime.</u>

Don't believe me? Watch Danny's behaviour, not for long, just for a few days. You'll see what I went through. And remember, don't bend over with him anywhere nearby; you'll regret it.

As well as being your wife — "in sickness and in health" — we are also business partners, and there are things that need to be discussed. I invested in your widget factory, after all, and have brought in more orders for you than ever before.

Could I ask just one favour? My little sister Blods is getting married on Saturday week. If we went to the wedding together, we could discuss these matters. If everything goes well, maybe you'd consider letting me come home, just to see how it goes. Please call me here soon.

I love you, honeybunch.

Mildred

Danny's mouth was hanging open slackly, a thousand competing horrors crowding in on his mind. He was trembling uncontrollably. The whole letter looked as if it had been written in nasty brownish-red ink. It was the colour of dried blood. Then he realized, with a jolt of fear, that the underlined sections were highly significant. That much was obvious from the things he'd done already as a result of the Zero Hex. And his final doom was even more horrible than he could possibly have imagined.

<u>It will all end for Danny with a spell behind bars. And the moment he's alone behind bars, he'll be lost to a life of crime.</u>

Danny's antisocial behaviour would see to it that he was put behind bars. And once he was alone, his life would be in ruins. Danny groaned in absolute despair, and for the first time, felt like giving up. At least he now knew his dad was hexed too; that much was a comfort. "Terry, you must believe me about this", it had said, underlined. And his dad did, because of the hexed words he had read.

But what could Danny do about it? If he took the letter to his dad, he'd only get in yet more trouble for sneaking about and putting his nose into someone's private correspondence. Danny didn't want to do anything to rile his father still further. It might just be the final nail in his coffin.

Clutching the letter, Danny went back to his room and lay on his bed, hopelessness consuming him. Then, in a last fit of desperation, he ripped savagely at the pages, until the hex letter lay in tiny pieces next to him. He closed his eyes, gasping. When he opened them a moment later, the pages were magically, terribly, whole once again.

Chapter 9

In Aunt Mildred's Suite

THROUGH HIS GLOOM, Danny gradually became aware of a familiar voice outside his window. It was Imogen calling him from the garden below, as planned. Danny opened the window and clambered down the drainpipe. "You won't get into trouble, will you?" said Danny as he landed heavily, his breath making great ragged swirls in the air.

"Don't worry, Mum's cool," Imogen replied. "Thinks I'm here with you – which I am. Hope she doesn't check up on me though because your dad or Aunt Mildred will say I'm not. Which is not really fair when you think about it, because I am! Complicated, isn't it?"

"Stop gibbering," said Danny. "There's something I need to tell you."

Imogen looked around nervously. "Where's Cuddles?"

"Not here. At the vet's, I think," said Danny.

"Listen," said Imogen. "Mildred's not going to be in her hotel suite tonight. I was hanging around reception and heard her and the manager, Smurthwaite, say so. And this is the best bit, Da—"

"There's quite a lot I need to tell you first," Danny interrupted. He retrieved the hex letter from his back pocket and handed it to her. "I think you'd better read this before I turn into a real criminal."

Imogen looked into Danny's frightened eyes, and then down at the hex letter, pursing her lips the further she read.

"These underlined parts are words of power," said

Danny, trying to keep his voice even, pointing at the letter. "*Pearls of wower* as Cyril Spectre used to call them in his books. 'Mark my words' is the clue – see it there? So the underlined bits dictate what I'll do, like kicking my dad up the backside," Danny said, his voice rising. "And something in this stinking thing's going to see me arrested, put behind bars, and…and—"

"Shush, Danny," Imogen said, putting her hand over his mouth to quieten him. "At least we know who made the Zero Hex now. We mustn't panic," she continued soothingly, although her voice was shaking. "We've got to make sure we recognize the tiniest little clue when it comes along."

"But what are we going to do?" Danny insisted.

"I've got a plan," said Imogen. "But first things first. She rummaged around in one of the deep pockets of her thick overcoat and produced a warm, tinfoil parcel. "I thought you might need this."

Danny took the parcel and unwrapped it to reveal several slices of roast lamb, a roast potato and some carrots. "Oh, you're an absolute legend," he said, beginning to eat hungrily. "What's this plan?" he continued thickly, wiping mint sauce off his lips.

"Well," said Imogen. "This is the good bit. It's taken me four nights of sneaking about in the cold, but I've got something big from my investigations at The Six Gold Stars." Imogen's eyes were shining with fierce excitement. "I heard Smurthwaite on the phone telling someone he's quitting his job to go overseas with Mildred but isn't quite sure when yet. So it's urgent, Danny. If we don't find out how to break the hex before she goes…" Imogen's worried eyes met Danny's. He nodded, with a grim expression on his face. After a short, serious silence she continued. "Apparently, before they can go, she needs one final thing…"

The curtains to the living room hadn't yet been drawn and the pair saw Aunt Mildred inside, hunting frantically through cupboards and drawers.

"I still don't get it," Danny said impatiently.

"Look," Imogen said, pointing.

Aunt Mildred was removing cushions from the settee, searching.

"She's looking for the one last thing she needs," said Imogen. "And she seems to think it's in your house."

Danny stared back at her, open-mouthed. "What could it be?" he whispered, his voice quivering.

"Don't know," said Imogen. "It could be the hex letter," she added, and Danny nodded vigorously in agreement. "But let's stay focused here. I suggest we search Mildred's hotel suite for more information, for anything that might help us defeat the hex. I'll meet you at The Six Gold Stars in an hour. What's the time now?" She squinted to read her watch. "That'll be ten-thirty. Smurthwaite's thrown me out once already, by the way. He actually caught me behind the reception counter checking out the keys! It was very embarrassing. So I'll have to act as the decoy while you pinch the key to Mildred's suite…"

"Great idea," said Danny. "We can…uh-oh! Aunt Mildred's left the lounge. Got to go." He clambered up the drainpipe quicker than a rat and slithered back into his room.

Barely a heartbeat later Aunt Mildred swung open Danny's bedroom door. "Who were you talking to?" she demanded.

"Just myself," Danny blurted out, moving away from

the window. "Just little old me." Aunt Mildred crossed the room in three strides and peered suspiciously into the darkness outside.

Danny held his breath. At last, Aunt Mildred moved away from the window and he could breathe again. She left him with a nasty threat: "And if that soup's not finished the next time I come upstairs, I'll pour it down your throat myself."

Aunt Mildred spent a lot of time on the telephone after that. He could hear her voice faintly in the downstairs hallway. Danny heard her mention the "meeting tonight". He deduced that most of the calls were overseas as she kept asking for the time and what sort of weather they were having. Soon afterwards he heard Aunt Mildred's car backing down the driveway and racing off into the night.

At around ten o' clock Dad came in and questioned Danny about whether he'd been snooping in the study as he'd lost something. When Danny denied it, trying not to look guilty, Dad said a curt "Lights out in five minutes"

and left the room. As soon as Dad's footfalls receded, Danny put on his sneakers and his school jacket (with the precious photograph from his mum still safely tucked into its left-hand pocket), opened his window as quietly as he could and clambered back down the drainpipe.

A thick mist had descended since Danny was last outside. He moved carefully across the back garden and went to open the garage's side door, cursing when he found it locked. His bicycle was inside. The large front doors to the double-garage were automated and could only be opened by the remote control and that was in the lounge with Dad. He would have to walk.

As bright lights flared in the mist, Danny was dazzled suddenly. It was Aunt Mildred's sports car roaring back into the front drive. He ducked down behind some bushes. Aunt Mildred climbed out of the car.

Danny crouched so still that his whole body ached. He watched her as she talked into her mobile phone. He cowered down a fraction lower.

"I'm still hoping to leave on Wednesday," she was saying. "But I've *got* to find it first. Danny's... Eh? I can't ask the brat for it, you fool. Don't want him to know."

Danny was beginning to wonder if it *was* the hex letter that she was looking for. He couldn't believe anything he had would be important enough to hold up Aunt Mildred's plans. By now she was on the front doorstep, her back to him. The conversation seemed to have changed tack.

"...my sister's. So see you at the castle tomorrow... the best fireworks... blood and thunder, I said to her. You can have jewel-encrusted elephants if you want. We've got the money. Okay, bye." She hung up.

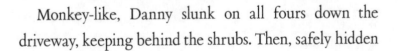

Monkey-like, Danny slunk on all fours down the driveway, keeping behind the shrubs. Then, safely hidden in the mist, he sprinted down the road to his rendezvous with Imogen.

Danny and Imogen met by the small fountain in the forecourt of The Six Gold Stars. Acting as innocently as they could, they walked towards the hotel's front doors.

Danny paused as they reached the entrance. A brightly lit reception area lay beyond that. "I assume that slimy-looking weasel at reception is Smurthwaite?" he said, pointing.

"You've got it!" said Imogen, grinning. "And directly behind him are the keys. Mildred's is in the top row, furthest left. Don't worry about the security guard. He's always asleep in his chair. Now, I'll run in and out again and when Smurthwaite comes after me, you nip in, grab the key and head straight for the lift. Go to the top floor. I'll give Smurthwaite the slip and meet you upstairs. You'll know it's me. I'll give three quick knocks on the door, followed by two slow ones."

Danny gave Imogen an admiring look. "Great plan! Have you thought of everything?"

"We won't know that until it's over," Imogen replied

with a grimace. "My insides are going round and round like a cement mixer on top speed. Wish me luck," she said.

"Good luck," Danny whispered and Imogen slunk into the hotel. He watched the action unfold like an old-fashioned silent movie: Imogen coolly approaching the front desk and picking up Smurthwaite's pen. The lazy look up from the man, and the flicker of recognition in his eyes. The lunge and grab at Imogen's arm, and her twisting free and running away, waving the pen about comically. Smurthwaite, gesticulating and mouthing, "Stop her! Stop! Stop, thief!"

Suddenly, it was silent no longer. Imogen burst out of the door and tore past him, Smurthwaite in close pursuit, yelling at the top of his voice.

Danny slipped inside, and with a thrill of terror found he'd walked straight into the arms of a giant security guard.

"Who are you?" the man demanded. So much for him being asleep in his chair, Danny thought wryly.

"I'm, er…nobody. The action's out there," said Danny, gesturing vaguely outside. "Someone stole the manager's pen, that's all. Can't be worth any more than fifty pence. He took off after her. Quite funny, really." Danny smiled weakly.

The security guard looked relieved and stern at the same time. "Which way did they go?" Danny pointed in exactly the wrong direction. The guard rushed out.

Racing behind the reception counter, Danny grabbed Aunt Mildred's room key from its hook and dived straight into a waiting lift. It whisked him up to the top floor where the doors opened again as a bell gave a loud *ping*. He ran down the corridor and soon found Aunt Mildred's suite. Fitting the key in the door, he went inside.

As soon as he turned the lights on, Danny knew it was hers, recognizing the large suitcases in the corner. He looked around with renewed wonder. He knew Aunt Mildred was rich – she seemed to own businesses all over the place – but she must have even more money than he realized, to be able to afford a suite like this. It had chandeliers, a grand piano, priceless antique furniture, Old Masters on the walls and a little marble pool on the balcony. A special enclosure had been hastily constructed for Cuddles in the sunken tiled section in the middle of the vast room. Above the doors was draped a great banner with golden tassels at the ends, proclaiming "S.L.A.Y.". But for all the luxury the place had a stale, unpleasant smell.

Double doors led through to a sumptuous dining area, dominated by a long, elaborate table of shiny wood laid out with silver cutlery and plates with opals round the edges. For some reason the foul stink – that he recognized now as *eau de hyena* – was stronger in there. With a snort of disgust, he pulled the doors closed.

Danny went over to a little antique table and started rummaging through the papers stacked there. A shimmering movement in the air caught his eye. Something was hovering near the ceiling. Looking up he saw immediately that it was something magical. It was fang-shaped and evil-looking, as black as the inside of a tomb, with grinning skulls and forks of lightning tattooed onto it. It tapered to a point as sharp as a rapier – a nib with dried, brownish-red poison ink around it. It was the hex pen.

Danny's heart gave a jump. Perhaps he could snap the hex pen in two. Would that destroy the hex, or make things worse? No, he decided, it wouldn't make things worse. I'm going to break it. Clambering on a chair, Danny reached out and made a grab for the evil thing. His hand passed straight through it.

Defeated again, he thought. Maybe that was part of its wicked magic. Once it had been used, perhaps it reverted to its spirit form and couldn't be touched? Frustrated, he bit down on the temptation to scream.

He felt like giving up, but the thought of a spell behind bars spurred him on. He carried on searching Aunt Mildred's suite.

As he cast about there was a thunderous knock at the door. It certainly wasn't the secret knock he and Imogen had agreed upon. Just as he was fleeing towards the balcony, he heard Imogen's frantic hiss from the other side of the door. "Danny! Danny! Open up! Quick! Danny!"

Racing over, he let her in. Imogen stumbled inside and

tumbled onto the floor. "Whew! That was close," she said, panting like a gazelle that had just felt the hot breath of a hungry lion breathing down its neck.

"What happened to the secret knock?" Danny demanded. "You nearly frightened me into my grave, hammering on the door like that."

Imogen's face was the colour of a beetroot. She held out her hand and Danny pulled her to her feet. "I reckon you'd forget all the niceties if you'd just been through what I have. Smurthwaite must be some sort of local sprint champion. You'd never believe it, would you?"

"And you'd never believe this, either, if you didn't see it with your own eyes." Danny pointed at the pen floating in midair, with a disgusted look on his face. "Not that we need any further proof that Aunt Mildred wrote the hex letter, but if we did, that's it. Trouble is, I can't even touch that stupid hex pen, let alone snap it. My hand just keeps passing straight through it."

"And I can't actually *see* it," said Imogen, peering at the ceiling with a puzzled expression.

Danny was dumbfounded. "You can't see it?"

"No, but look, let's not waste time on something you

can't touch and I can't even see. Smurthwaite's going to notice this room key's missing any minute. Let's have a quick look round and then get out of here, Danny."

The pair conducted a frantic search, hardly exchanging a word. After a few minutes Danny found a note on the corner of a newspaper that had been thrown into the bin. He read it out aloud. "Listen Imogen: 'S.L.A.Y. Extraord. Gen. Meet. Tonight, time change, now 11.30…P.S. HQ'. It's a clue, Imogen!"

Imogen rushed over and inspected the newspaper. "It's today's," she exclaimed. Then she looked at her watch. "It's nearly eleven! The meeting's in half an hour's time – but *where* is it? What's P.S. HQ?"

"Extraordinary general meeting," said Danny, looking thoughtful. "That's what Cyril was trying to tell me about."

"But P.S. HQ?" Imogen repeated, urgently.

"HQ obviously stands for headquarters," said Danny. "But P.S.? Postscript? Doesn't make sense, does it?"

"Maybe it's someone's name," said Imogen.

"Smurthwaite? Maybe the meeting's here," said Danny.

"Nah. His first name's Charles. I've heard people calling him it."

"Snodgrass?"

"Shirley."

"Is it really?" said Danny. "Got it!" he yelled some moments later, startling her. "P.S. stands for Peregrine Strauss, the principal. They must be meeting somewhere around his office – you know – where he and Aunt Mildred did that disappearing act! It's obvious, isn't it?"

"Nice work, Danny. Let's get over to the school."

As she headed for the door, Imogen noticed a slip of paper stuffed between the pages of the hotel's menu as if hurriedly hidden there. Curious, she slid it out of its hiding place and read what was printed on it.

"Eureka!" Imogen cried. "Check this out. It's a fax not more than two hours old." Danny dashed over and joined her.

They read it together:

The 7th Wessex Club's Flight Party:
Flight BR 129 to Parvatelli (Wed, April 23rd, 0900)
By the order of Mr. Julius Rapax

Badger, Emma, Mrs. (librarian)

Bogan-Swithens, William, Mr. (millionaire corporate banker)

Botfly, Bruce, Mr. (onion pickler)

Chowdhury, Malcolm, Mr. (builder)

Claxon, Enid, Miss (retired librarian)

Cloke, Mildred, Mrs. (millionaire businesswoman)

Daw, David, Mr. (policeman)

Fogerty, Joanne, Mrs. (teacher)

Fogerty, Timothy, Mr. (accountant)

Gander, Bertha, Mrs. (professional netball player)

Gander, Brian, Mr. (builder)

Lopez, Santiago, Mr. (don't ask)

Nankervis, John, Bp. (bishop)

Neville, Blodwyn, Miss (restaurateur)

Neville (Junior), Neville, Mr. (millionaire "Addictive Pizza" owner)

Perkins, Joy, Mrs. (biochemist)

Pernfors, Sven, Mr. (politician)

Plum, Alice, Mrs. (librarian)

Pobblebonk, "Froggie", Mr. (vet)

Ponsonby, Henry, Sir (nobility)

Porter, Katherine, Mrs. (teacher)

Porter, Sam, Mr. (teacher)

Robilliard, John, Mr. (teacher)

Singh, Sunil, Dr. (doctor)

Smurthwaite, Charles, Mr. (hotelier)

Snodgrass, Shirley, Miss (teacher)

Strauss, Peregrine, Mr. (school principal)

Strawberry, Quentin, Mr. (librarian)

Tartell, Phillip, Mr. (businessman)

Wiggie, Argell, Mr. (pamphlet writer)

*Please carry out instructions to the letter while on this trip. Failure will almost certainly result in death or serious injury.
Deaths on location this month:
Alfie Stringfellow (U.K.). Slobodan Bogdanovich (Croatia).

Mildred Cloke — United Kingdom president of S.L.A.Y.

They both finished reading at the same time and stared at one another. "This – this is big," Danny stuttered finally.

"This is scary," Imogen whispered, white-faced. "I count thirty people on this list."

"And I recognize most of the names," said Danny. "They're all locals."

"How big *is* this organization?" Imogen whispered.

"Huge! Look, this is the *Seventh* Wessex Club. That means there must be at least six others. And d'you know something else?" Danny went on. "There are *five* of our teachers listed here, *and* the principal. Doesn't surprise me to see Snotty Snodgrass there, but Mrs. Fogerty? I thought she was nice."

"That's just the top of the ice cream, Danny," Imogen said, tapping the document excitedly. "Look, String Bean gets a mention down the bottom. Whatever they're up to doesn't sound like a Butlins holiday camp, does it?"

"But what *are* they all supposed to be doing?"

"Whatever it is, they're doing it in Parvatelli," said Imogen, pointing. "Where is that, by the way?"

"Don't know. We'll have to check," said Danny.

"You know the best bit?" said Imogen. "Look who's ordered it: Julius Rapax!"

"The guy with the same name as our school!" The revelations were crowding into Danny's mind like bats in a cave. Without thinking, he opened the doors to the dining room again.

Danny and Imogen saw them at the same time; a pair of evil yellow eyes peering from beneath a dining table. Slowly the eyes came towards them, and there stood Cuddles, rolling back its lips and revealing vicious fangs. Imogen screamed.

"Don't panic," said Danny. "I know how to handle this brute. You'll be all right. Back carefully towards the balcony. Trust me. I've lived with Cuddles. Tell me when you've got there." Cuddles took a step towards Danny, growling threateningly.

"I'm there," said Imogen after a few moments.

"You're going to have to climb down the drainpipe. It's not far down."

"It is if I slip. Anyway, what about you?"

"I'm coming," said Danny. He did a backwards shuffle towards the balcony. A quick glance behind him showed Imogen clambering over the edge, and just starting to climb down, clinging onto the drainpipe and a nearby tree.

The moment Danny looked away the beast lunged at him, snapping at his kneecaps with powerful jaws. Danny screamed, jumped backwards through the balcony doors, and stumbled. As he scrambled to his feet Cuddles advanced again.

This time the hyena had him cornered. Cuddles prepared to pounce. Suddenly, the door to the suite swung open with considerable force. The hotel manager,

Smurthwaite, and the security guard stood framed in the doorway. Cuddles turned and studied them briefly; then its cruel gaze turned back to Danny.

At the door to the suite, Smurthwaite barked out his orders. "Winston, get downstairs and catch the girl. I've got this one cornered…"

Plummeting ten metres downwards seemed more appealing to Danny than facing the wrath of Aunt Mildred, or a police escort to the nearest cells, and then, *goodnight*. Besides, being caught would mean not making it to the S.L.A.Y. meeting. No way! He moved to the edge of the balcony. The awning above the hotel's entrance would break his fall, wouldn't it? But it was a long way down…

Cuddles pounced and Danny vaulted the metal handrail. The hyena's teeth closed over Danny's backside and came away with a leather patch that said "Cyril Spectre Spells Magic". The snarling beast spat out its meagre prize in disgust.

In the same second Danny flew through the air. His arms and legs flailed furiously for a moment before a curious calmness came over him and he felt as weightless as a white, gossamer-stranded dandelion seed…

Something was tickling his face. It was a lock of Imogen's hair. She was looking down at him with a worried expression. "Are you all right? You sort of bounced and then managed to land on your feet, I think. Then you fell over."

Danny rubbed his eyes. Then he ran his hand over his left-hand jacket pocket. It gave a satisfying crinkle. Yes, the photograph was still there.

"You bounced off the awning," Imogen said, looking at it doubtfully. "You can now officially add superhero to your list of achievements." Danny was lying in the flowerbeds a few feet away. "Anyway let's go," she finished.

"THE SECURITY GUARD'S COMING!" Danny yelled suddenly. They sprang to their feet and ran off into the misty night together.

Tunnel Visions

HAVING SPRINTED all the way to school, Danny and Imogen clambered over the locked school gates and stole across the unlit forecourt. Even in the darkness they could make out some shadowy figures in the distance, going swiftly into Principal Strauss's office.

"Bingo," whispered Imogen.

Danny smiled at her. "Let's hang round here until they're all inside. We're going to have to find out where they're going without getting caught."

Some minutes later they decided to make their move. Danny and Imogen crept across the playground and ducked behind the wall of the principal's building, checking for guards. "All clear," whispered Danny.

He put his ear to the door of the principal's office. There was no sound. After a nervous glance at Imogen, he opened it. The office was completely deserted.

Astonished despite herself, Imogen whispered, "How can that many people have vanished?" Danny shrugged.

The pair scouted around for a hidden exit. Finally, Danny stopped before a painting in the corner of the office. "Look at this Imogen." At first glance it depicted Santa Claus soaring across the sky with reindeer pulling his sleigh. But a closer inspection revealed that he was about a metre above the sleigh with a look of terror on his face, as if they'd hit sudden turbulence. In a similarly precarious position, toys were spilling from a sack.

"I think it's meant to be a joke," Danny said uncertainly.

"Not a very funny one. It's horrible," said Imogen, joining him. "Wait a minute, though. S.L.A.Y. ... Sleigh...?"

"If you turned the picture upside down," said Danny, "Santa and the toys would be falling towards the ground and the reindeer and the sleigh would be spinning out of control." He gasped. "That's it! That's the way it's meant to be!"

Danny turned the picture around. There was a clicking sound; a section of the wall slid aside and a small, bare, windowless room with meagre light revealed itself. No members of S.L.A.Y. were there. Danny looked at Imogen triumphantly. She gave him a silent thumbs-up. But as they peered into the gloom, their joy was replaced by fear.

"Let's get it over with, shall we?" Danny suggested. As they stepped inside the room, the wall slid smoothly back into place behind them. Imogen shrieked. Danny clutched her hand.

After a moment, Imogen said, "It's okay, look. We're in a lift. There are the buttons, up and down."

Danny pressed down. They descended for what felt like a very long time. There was a slight shudder at their feet when they arrived. The door slid open once more, revealing a long dark tunnel with a patch of red light in the distance.

"Can you hear something?" asked Imogen.

"Yeah, come on." They padded across the dusty, tattered old carpet. Along the entire length of the gloomy corridor, stacked against the walls all the way up to the ceiling, were boxes. The pair paused to investigate. Imogen opened one of the boxes and flinched as something brushed her face.

"It's just cobwebs," said Danny, wiping the dusty strands from her face.

Just then the lift made a rattling noise. Danny and Imogen ducked behind a pile of boxes. The lift door opened and Smurthwaite hurried past and disappeared down the corridor with a harrassed look on his face.

Cautiously the pair came out of hiding. Imogen continued investigating the boxes. "Look, Cyril Clegg books!"

"I recognize that one," said Danny. "It's that timeless classic, *The Noise of Every Car Engine is Slightly Different*."

"There are one hundred and forty-eight books in this box alone. See? It says so on the outside." Imogen gazed at the piles of boxes stretching out in both directions. "So – so there must be millions of them here."

"Enough to poison the *germinations* of generations of children," Danny replied, quoting Cyril Spectre. "Come on. Let's go."

Imogen closed the box and they moved on, Danny in the lead. At the end of the corridor the sign on the imposing double doors said: Any Children Caught Here Will Be Donated To Our Laboratories For Scientific Experiments.

Swallowing, Danny peered into the brightly lit room

from the relative safety of the dingy corridor – and gasped in amazement.

There was something darkly majestic about the place. Dozens of candelabra cut from blood-red glass hung from the ceiling and the thousands of individual droplets artfully formed the dagger-like S.L.A.Y. insignia. Heavy crimson velvet drapes were everywhere, all embroidered with the same sinister crest.

The members of S.L.A.Y. sat at ornate tables, the surfaces of which depicted maps of the country in great detail. Little red lights twinkled on them.

Danny saw Malicia Clegg at a podium on the stage. She was peering at some large folded blueprints. On a screen at the back of the stage was another enormous map of the world, with innumerable tiny red lights twinkling all over it. On either side, stacks of boxes were partially hidden behind curtains.

As Principal Strauss mounted the stage, Malicia put the papers down, and he picked them up without looking at her. She took a seat by herself at a table below.

Danny whispered to Imogen, "I can see Aunt Mildred. She's at the front table. She told Dad she was playing bridge tonight! Come to think of it, she's been saying that for years. Now Smurthwaite's whispering something to her – it'll be about us, no doubt."

Imogen looked over Danny's shoulder. "Who's the oafish fellow sat behind Aunt Mildred?"

"I recognize him, but can't think where from. And look. My Year Four teacher, Mrs. Fogerty, is with Snodgrass at that table further back. Every one of them's wearing a S.L.A.Y. armband," Danny added disgustedly.

"Shush. It's starting," said Imogen.

On stage, Principal Strauss spoke into the microphone. "Welcome to the bunker. Thank you for your attendance at this extraordinary general meeting. As the head of the Seventh Wessex chapter of S.L.A.Y., it is my privilege and my pleasure to introduce to you someone whose international duties are increasingly robbing us of her brilliant presence. It is, of course, the finest president of S.L.A.Y. this country has ever had! Our very own Mildred Cloke!" There was thunderous applause as Aunt Mildred ascended the stage.

"CHILDREN!" she spat. "Horrible, nasty, selfish, childish brutes." A roar of approval greeted this.

Her voice took on a mocking quality. "'Mummy, I want this. No, I don't want this now. I want that. It's not fair. He hit me...'" Her tone became cold and sharp again as her eyes roved the room, seeking the expression on every face. "Why do they think they can make demands? They're nobodies! A sub-class! They should be our slaves!" There was rapturous applause again.

"They don't earn the money!" she went on. "We do. They don't get to vote. We do. Who bought the television that they feel they can monopolize? We did. And what about that strange, fantastical nonsense they read that fills their heads with idle daydreams? If you suggest something practical like a manual on bee-keeping, they look at you as if you're the one with the problem. In an ideal world, until you turn twenty-one years of age, you wouldn't be allowed to speak unless you were spoken to first!" Spontaneous cheers erupted.

Aunt Mildred waited until they had subsided before continuing, "But enough of this jolly banter. The reason I have gathered you here tonight is to tell you all something that you will scarcely believe. I won't blame any of you if you can't take it in at first." She proceeded to tell the stunned audience about how Danny and Cyril Spectre had hexed her and turned her into a purple-bearded ape-woman. "Fortunately, after that, my dead grandfather, Neville Neville, came to my aid from *the other side*," she continued. "He is now a Hobblegob from the realm of Gloom, and he hates my stepson, too. He gave me a magical and deliciously evil hex pen, with instructions on how to write a letter putting a Zero Hex on that throbbing carbuncle, Danny, making him act the giddy goat. Neville Neville removed my own hexes, too. I'd like to think this was out of family loyalty, but suspect it is for reasons of his own. From what I can understand, spirits normally only assist us to further their own ends. Hobblegobs will always be beyond our control. I know it's unbelievable but—"

"Danny made a goat of himself in my very classroom! It must be true!" Miss Snodgrass yelled out with a screech of laughter. Everyone in the room joined in with her mirth. Danny looked on, fuming.

"It is only a matter of time before the Zero Hex sees to it that Danny has a spell behind bars!" Aunt Mildred roared triumphantly. "And the instant he's left alone in that terrible cage, he'll be lost to a life of crime!" The S.L.A.Y. members let out a spontaneous cheer, exchanging gloating looks. A few hugged each other in their excitement. Malicia hugged herself.

Outside, Danny looked over, queasily, at Imogen.

Imogen looked at him sympathetically. "It's the most terrible thing I've ever heard," she whispered.

"Even for S.L.A.Y.," continued Aunt Mildred, "this is a most satisfying result. I had almost crushed Danny's spirit before, but I was thwarted. Now I have struck back with the powerful Zero Hex. The absolute subjugation of every child's spirit and imagination will always be our main purpose. Quell imagination and you quell freedom. And the quelling of freedom is the root to all power!

"But the moment Danny's doom is sealed and the hex

pen disappears back to the realm of Gloom, our memories will be wiped of all events connected with it."

There were incredulous murmurs around the room. "But surely," Smurthwaite called out, "I'll never forget the purple-bearded ape-woman? We're still fumigating!"

"Thank you, Smurthwaite," snapped Aunt Mildred. "In your mind you'll remember her as a sideshow freak, and in mine I will put it down to a temporary malady or tropical disease from which I've fully recovered. The spirits themselves don't wish to be remembered," she went on. "Shirley, you will have some memory of Danny acting the goat in your classroom; but only within the normal bounds of a child fooling about."

"Can anything go wrong with your plan?" asked Miss Snodgrass.

"Nothing!" barked Aunt Mildred. "The Zero Hex will only be annulled if I burn the hex letter so that every word is gone." The members of the audience looked around, grinning. "Only then would the pact with my Hobblegob grandfather be broken."

Danny and Imogen's eyes met, hope suddenly blazing and crackling like fire in the space between them.

"But even the torturing of Danny with the Zero Hex is a side issue to the grand scheme," said Aunt Mildred. "Julius Rapax told me some years ago to infiltrate the Cloke residence. Julius has been working on his plans to enslave all children for years, and, as you know, I have had the honour of helping him in some of these noble enterprises. And tonight we are ready to reveal our most top-secret plan! You are all sworn to silence. Should any of you present tonight reveal even a word of what I'm about to tell you, then you will discover the delights of my charming pet, Cuddles." There was an awed hush as Mildred glared at her audience with beady eyes. Then she continued.

"WE WILL DEVELOP A SPRAY THAT MAKES CHILDREN FORGET! Forget about wonderful books, and the beauty of nature, and growing up into adults that dare to dream. We will extinguish their life spark!

"Look at the little red dots on the maps at your tables. Each one is a secret S.L.A.Y. headquarters. Every time you come here the dots have multiplied. Only yesterday I opened up a new secret bunker at a school in Aberdeen, 'The Julius Rapax School – 2nd Aberdeenshire'. Now all our sympathizers living in the area will see the name and pay the principal a visit. S.L.A.Y. teachers and librarians can apply for a position knowing the principal is on their side. And look here," she said with a sweep of her arm to what lay behind her. "Look at this great map of the world. See how we are advancing. Luxembourg and Swaziland joined us for the first time this week. We have done all of this without the spray. With it, we will rule the world!"

"Such a spray's not possible!" called out a man near the back. "I say this whole thing's getting out of control."

"You fool, Gander!" roared Aunt Mildred, her eyes glittering. "Must you always think so small? I tell you it is not only possible, it has already begun. Julius Rapax has given me his permission to begin work on what will henceforth be known as the Memory-Numbing Spray.

"Tonight we welcome a new member to S.L.A.Y. She is the country's finest biochemist. Now we have her, let us welcome Joy Perkins!"

There was a scattering of polite applause as a plump blonde-haired woman got to her feet and waved at everyone self-consciously before plunking herself back down.

"How much will this spray cost?" Gander persisted.

"We're giving Joy ten million pounds to develop the prototype and an antidote for any S.L.A.Y. member who might otherwise suffer some mild symptoms," said Aunt Mildred calmly. There were moans of scepticism at this. "Julius Rapax has agreed to give us the ten million when I have got a final piece of information he wants from my stepson Danny, and we have made a successful delivery to Julius."

Outside, in the hallway, Danny and Imogen exchanged a look. Now, at last, they were going to find out what it was that Aunt Mildred was searching for. But just at that moment she was interrupted again.

"Can I ask why we're all going to Parvatelli?" said Miss Snodgrass. "I've heard rumours that we're trying to catch spirits or some such nonsense."

Holding up her hand for silence, Aunt Mildred said, "Shirley, I promise you will be informed of everything the moment you get off the plane. As will everyone else…"

The stocky little man called Brian Gander sprang to his feet. "But Mildred – ten million pounds? We could build ten Cyril Clegg libraries with that. And ten million's just to develop the stuff. That's without a single child being sprayed. How are you going to pump enough of it into the atmosphere to brainwash one kid in Nettle Bottom, let alone the whole world? And how much will it cost to pump the spray out around the entire world?"

"A hundred billion pounds, Brian."

Gander spluttered and his false teeth hit the table with a crash. "A hun're meemum mouns?"

"Better add another two hundred to that estimate to get your teeth fixed," Aunt Mildred said with a cruel smile. "I have never failed any of you before. I believe that we have three years of hard work ahead of us before 'The Chimneys' are operable but tonight, for the first time, you can see a model." Everyone in the room gazed about expectantly.

In the draughty corridor, Danny and Imogen gave each other a quick, nervous glance, wondering what was coming next.

Taking the blueprints from Principal Strauss – who still stood just behind her – Aunt Mildred unfolded one of them, placed it on the podium and waved a small black control box across the large sheet.

Immediately a slithering, scuttling sound filled the air and countless shiny silver metallic robots the size and shape of scorpions poured out of boxes at the back of the stage, dropped lightly to the floor below and, without slowing down, spread out across the room. Everyone recoiled.

"Widgets," Danny whispered to Imogen. "Dad's widgets. But there are so many of them. Thousands."

"What do widgets do?" Imogen said in a low voice.

"They perform set tasks in places where people can't go," Danny explained, watching the widgets spinning frenziedly on top of one another in great piles. "They have the task programmed into a microchip. They can do almost anything, anywhere. You know, like deep underwater, in the airless vacuum of outer space, in volcanoes and other poisonous atmospheres. They collect samples and gather information and fix things. Normally he gets orders for one or two at a time, maybe ten at the most."

Imogen looked at the widgets more closely as they buzzed about like an infestation. They had two interlocking wheels in each corner as sharp as razor blades. The narrow joints between them were capable of bending or folding at any angle. Many of the widgets were glowing with different colours, all in a dull metallic sheen. Each of the eight wheels of every individual widget interlocked with those of its companions in a glittering flurry until, at last, they were still.

On stage, Aunt Mildred held up the blueprints triumphantly. "Behold!" She gestured to the astonishing sight that had now grown up all around them, towering right to the ceiling; enormous chimneys – all interconnected by a complex series of mock underground tunnels.

Some of the S.L.A.Y. members leaned back and gawped up at the stupendous structures soaring above them. Others were looking down at the complicated tunnels by their feet, which were criss-crossing under and across the tables.

"Julius and I were talking fondly about how children were used as chimney sweeps in Victorian times," said Aunt Mildred, shattering the awed silence that had fallen across the room. "And then I came up with the idea of a thousand great chimneys keeping the children of the world enslaved. We realized that giant chimneys pumping out Memory-Numbing Spray should be our great work. If you give me your support, we will give you the world."

Everyone in the room leaped up and cheered and clapped and stamped. Aunt Mildred gazed back at them triumphantly. Slowly the noise died down and the crowd resumed their seats.

"How will this spray target children, and not adults?" a man called out.

"Ah, now that's the really clever bit, Bruce," said Aunt Mildred and the way her lip curled upwards to reveal pointed teeth made her look like a jackal. "It punishes them for being what they are - children. The smaller you are, the more it will affect you. It's a simple matter of ratios."

"That's outrageous!" squeaked a tiny little man called Argell Wiggie, his chin bouncing up and down on the tabletop in his fury.

"Calm yourself, Wiggie," said Aunt Mildred. "Remember, there will be an antidote for all S.L.A.Y. members."

"Will the chimneys be made of these widgets, Mildred?" asked Principal Strauss.

"Oh, no," said Aunt Mildred. "They were just helping with my demonstration tonight. But the widgets'll have several very important tasks. During the next couple of years their main one will be to sneak into the children's rooms at night and test out Joy's spray."

His false teeth returned to their accustomed place, Brian Gander alone had remained standing. He was smiling ecstatically, revealing a large chip in a front tooth. "Sso, all we've got to do iss go to Parvatelli," he whistled, "and finissh thiss ssecret tassk of yourss. And then Juliuss givess uss the ten million to get thiss ssecret sspray sstarted. You'd better tell uss how we're going to ssuccccceed in the tassk?"

"Like this, Brian." Aunt Mildred unfolded another blueprint, placed it on the podium and waved her control pad across it. Instantly, the great chimneys' structure collapsed with surprisingly little noise. Most of the widgets sprang back up on stage with grasshopper-like movements and disappeared into their boxes behind the curtains. In the meantime, the rest had formed a cage around Mr. Gander, who looked stunned. Everyone else applauded.

Danny's blood turned to ice. "Bars," he whispered to Imogen.

"I think we'd better go."

"Yes, I…" Danny took a last look inside and saw, unmistakably, that Malicia Clegg had spotted him. She shot up from her chair and started across the room.

"She's seen us," he hissed, tugging Imogen's arm. "She's coming over! Run! Run!" The pair ran for their lives back down the corridor. Imogen pressed the button to call the lift. The doors opened smoothly and they sprang inside.

"There she is," panted Danny, as Malicia Clegg tore towards them with a surprising turn of speed.

Imogen was frantically pressing the lift buttons, and at last the doors slid closed behind them. "Did you see her?" asked Danny, his breathing coming in ragged gasps.

"No," said Imogen, concentrating furiously on trying to get the lift to work. Finally, it began to move upwards.

When they reached the ground floor, they dashed across the principal's study, through the outer office and out into the night.

"At least we're alive," Imogen said as they clambered over the school gates. "I wasn't sure we'd make it out of there." They kept running until they were sure they weren't being pursued.

"I thought Malicia had spotted me," Danny said, looking back in puzzlement. "I thought there might have been more of a fuss. Why weren't the others after us too? It doesn't make sense."

Imogen could barely put one foot in front of the other. "I've no idea. But we'd better get home. We'll meet tomorrow morning at detention and work out what to do next."

Danny reached for the hex letter in his pocket. "We've got to get Aunt Mildred to burn this," he said. "It's the only way I can stop my whole life being ruined." He knew it would be easier said than done, and his heart was heavy as they said goodbye at a street corner where their paths divided.

"Oh, I forgot to tell you," said Imogen. "Remember to cover your bum up if anyone is walking behind you. Cuddles has taken an awfully big chunk out of your jeans…"

Chapter 11

The Unhappily Married Couple

DANNY LAY AWAKE in blood-chilling dread, waiting for Aunt Mildred's car to pull up in the driveway. When he finally heard her come home, he waited for the sound of her feet thundering up the stairs, followed by the dazzle of his bedroom light and her harsh voice roaring accusations about spying on her meeting.

He was both relieved and perplexed when none of this happened and the house remained quiet.

It was hard to work out where the nightmares began and the dark memories ended, but everything floated about in Danny's mind with the clarity of gravy until he fell asleep.

When daylight flooded the room, Danny felt incredibly tired. His brain was working at the speed of a tortoise about to hibernate. He looked about him and saw his ripped jeans lying in a heap on the floor where he must have dropped them the night before. Dimly, he realized he'd have to hide them. They were incriminating evidence of his escapades. He scrunched them into a ball and threw them into the back of his wardrobe, tossing his jacket over the top. There, that should do it, he thought. He grabbed some other clothes, and scrambled into them.

Stumbling downstairs, he went outside, retrieved his bicycle from the garage and headed out to serve his detention. There was no sign of Dad or Aunt Mildred anywhere.

It's lucky the Zero Hex got me that punishment,

Danny realized with a wry smile. Or I'd not be able to catch up with Imogen.

As it happened, nearly half the school had a detention – a fairly normal occurrence – so they all gathered in the assembly hall. Danny joined Imogen at their usual seats, near the back. Mrs. Fogerty was sitting at a small desk on stage, watching over them, looking exhausted.

"No wonder she looks tired, the traitor," said Danny, whispering behind his hand. He looked around. There were over three hundred pupils in the great hall. Chopper Chowdhury was two rows back, and Danny was careful not to catch his eye.

"What do you think it is of yours that's worth ten million pounds to the world leader of S.L.A.Y.?" Imogen whispered to Danny.

"I don't know. The ten million's not going to do me much good though, is it?" said Danny. Another thought brought a surge of hope with it. "I could tell Aunt Mildred that I know she's looking for something of mine worth ten million, and that I'll give it to her if she burns the hex letter! I'll tell her I'll destroy whatever it is if she doesn't."

Imogen looked unconvinced. "You could give it a go, I suppose. But I reckon you've got as much chance of her agreeing to that as asking a tyrannosaurus to sign an autograph book!"

Tarquin Botfly, who'd just sat down next to them, laughed. "Yeah, a T-Rex couldn't sign anything with those tiny little arms!"

A sudden, frosty look from Mrs. Fogerty cut short any further conversation. Imogen gave Tarquin a sour, sidelong glance. Then she whispered to Danny, "I'll tell you what, as soon as we've finished detention we're going to slip away and set fire to this letter."

"No, that won't work," said Danny. "Remember what Aunt Mildred said in the bunker? It has to be her that burns it."

Imogen's brow became increasingly furrowed as she rattled off idea after idea; her determined look soon replaced with one of desperation. "Okay – okay," she said, coming up with her twentieth suggestion. "We hollow out a candle and put the hex letter inside, hand it to Mildred and get her to light it."

But it always came back to the same problem. Aunt

Mildred wasn't remotely likely to do anything that Danny, or even his dad asked her, especially if it involved fire. It was too obvious. Danny was pointing this out when the bell sounded for the end of detention.

They trudged out of the hall, looking defeated. "Why don't you hang on to this," said Danny, handing Imogen the hex letter. "At least it'll be safe with you. We'd never break the pact if we lost the letter."

Imogen nodded and pocketed it.

"Sounds like you two have got problems," said Tarquin, as he walked past them, and then bit his lip. "Sorry. Couldn't help overhearing. But remember, if you ever need a hand, I'm your man." He hurried across the playground.

"Tarquin Botfly!" Imogen yelled after him, scandalized. Then, surprisingly, an eager look came across her face. "Tarquin!" she said, and hefting her large rucksack onto one shoulder, raced over to him. "Tarquin, hold up a minute…"

Walking into the kitchen with a quailing heart, Danny saw no sign of his dad. But Aunt Mildred was waiting for him. She looked up and fixed him with a gimlet eye.

"We're attending my little sister Blodwyn's wedding today," Aunt Mildred said, watching him closely for a reaction. "She's finally marrying that worthless oaf, Malcolm Chowdhury. Big Mal, everyone calls him."

Danny's first thought was one of relief. Aunt Mildred didn't seem to know, or care about Danny's trespassing and eavesdropping the night before. But it didn't make sense. Was it a trick? A trap?

Then Danny froze. Blodwyn! Aunt Mildred had said her little sister, *Blodwyn*. The woman talking to the vicar outside the churchyard last Sunday! He knew he'd recognized her. She had the same unpleasant features as Aunt Mildred. And Big Mal... Oh, no! Big Mal! Danny had called them the vulture and the rock ape, and barely escaped with his life. What would the happy couple do when they saw Danny at the wedding? He felt sure they wouldn't ask him to be a last-minute pageboy.

"I do believe," Aunt Mildred went on conversationally, "that Big Mal has a baby brother who'll be there. He goes to your school. Roger Chowdhury. He goes by the nickname of 'Chopper', so I'm told." Danny let out a little whimper. The flea-bitten baboon would be there as well! This was a nightmare.

"Vicar Nannish will be marrying the happy couple," Aunt Mildred continued remorselessly. Danny realized that all the people he'd upset, offended or insulted since being Zero Hexed were now being gathered together for the grand finale.

"Who else will be there?" Danny asked. If he was going to his doom he wanted to be prepared.

"Oh, let me see," said Aunt Mildred. "Mr. and Mrs. Fogerty, Mr. and Mrs. Gander, and my father will be there, of course. Miss Snodgrass and your principal..."

Danny wasn't listening any more. It was the wedding of two S.L.A.Y. members! The guests were the same people who were listed on the fax about the Seventh Wessex Club's Flight Party, gathered together to witness the happy day, the final humiliation of Danny Cloke.

"I've looked at all your clothes and I want you to wear this jacket." Aunt Mildred held up the one he always wore to school. "But your dad will have to buy you some new trousers because of *this*!" She removed from the front pocket of her pinafore a leather patch that said "Cyril Spectre Spells Magic" and slammed it down on the kitchen table.

Danny's heart lurched violently. Just then Dad appeared behind Aunt Mildred, his face stern, holding the ruined jeans Danny had tried to hide at the back of his wardrobe.

"A boy and a girl broke into my hotel suite late last night," Aunt Mildred continued, her voice rising shrilly. "The manager, Mr. Smurthwaite, gave me their descriptions. They sound like you and your little friend, Imogen. These cat burglars performed a spectacular escape, but not before Cuddles had relieved the boy of this patch," she said, picking it up and waving it in Danny's face. Her tone became soft with menace. "Honeybunch, pull those jeans round the right way and let's reunite them with this bit of cheap merchandise." Danny stood still, quaking with fear. This was the end. They'd lock him up in the deepest, darkest, most slimy-walled dungeon for this.

Time stood still as Dad tugged the jeans the right

way out. Finally he flipped them over on the table. Everyone stared in amazement. They were completely intact, sporting their own "Cyril Spectre Spells Magic" leather patch.

"Well, I'm pleased," Dad said, finally breaking the atmosphere of crackling electricity that had pervaded the kitchen, "that there's one piece of villainy this week that you weren't involved in, Danny."

Nodding dumbly, Danny glanced up at his dad, allowing himself to look away from the miracle that had occurred. Then Cyril's words came floating back to him, almost the last words he had spoken before disappearing back into his gravestone: *"I've replaced the patch, but I can do no more."*

Danny looked at Aunt Mildred. Her face was bright puce, a kaleidoscope of conflicting emotions. "I apologize, darling Danny," she said icily. "Let's say I make it up to you. I know you'd enjoy my sister's wedding more if your friend Imogen came along. Would you like that?" Danny nodded; realizing this might be the very last chance for them to be together.

If he hadn't been so jumpy and exhausted, maybe he

would have spotted the jaws of the trap opening. Aunt Mildred picked up the telephone as Dad went back upstairs. After making the necessary arrangements with Imogen's mum, and boasting about the fact that it was to be held at a castle, and that the finest fireworks ever to be seen in these parts were going to be a feature, she put the phone down and turned back to Danny. "Mr. Smurthwaite, the manager of the hotel where I'm staying, will also be there." Now Danny realized the terrible mistake he had made.

"I don't know how you managed the switch with the jeans," Aunt Mildred hissed, studying him closely with tiny eyes that never seemed to blink. "But your luck's just run out. Smurthwaite wasn't confident of positively identifying you at the hotel last night, and that security guard is so useless I don't think he'd recognize his own face if you showed it to him. But Smurthwaite's sure that he can identify Imogen. A young red-haired girl with striking looks, so he says. She's been snooping around all week, he reckons. It's a pound to a penny that the police will become involved. *It'll be a spell behind bars for you, Danny.*"

Danny was desperate. It was time to lay down all his cards. "I know everything you're doing!" he shouted wildly. "I mean about Neville Neville and the hex letter and...everything," he finished lamely as Aunt Mildred's fierce stare melted all hope within him.

"So what?" She shrugged. "There's nothing you can do about it. Possessing the facts and being able to do something about them are two quite different things. Anyway, you don't know how to break the hex. And I'm absolutely sure you haven't guessed how truly terrifying your final fate is, because if you had, you'd be unable to speak. You'd just be a mass of quivering jelly on the floor."

Shaking, Danny looked into Aunt Mildred's cold eyes for clues, then decided to gamble. "I'll give you the thing that's holding you up," Danny said, "if you stop the Zero Hex." Seeing that Aunt Mildred looked unmoved, he added, "I didn't switch the jeans. Magic's at work. I'd say Cyril's about to make a comeback."

"You may have been helped with the jeans," said Aunt Mildred, "but that won't affect your fate. Besides," she added, leering horribly, "you forgot your jacket, didn't you?"

Instantly, Danny realized. The jacket he'd thrown on top of his jeans in the wardrobe. She had his photograph – his precious photograph – of the Long-tailed Pink Polka-dotted Home-wrecking Cuckoo. How could he have forgotten that he had to keep it safe?

Aunt Mildred laughed cruelly. "The final piece of the puzzle came into my possession while you were serving your school detention. Now go to the outside freezer and feed Cuddles the zebra foal's head. It's a special treat."

"Special treat?" said Danny dully, his mind full of the disaster.

"Cuddles has done a good job. You must've got lucky back at the hotel, that's all. Next time you won't escape so lightly." She strode out of the kitchen and upstairs.

"Tarquin's machine worked," Imogen whispered to Danny as everyone gathered at Upon-the-Sod Church for Big Mal and Blodwyn's wedding. "The copy of the hex letter is just perfect."

Danny looked at her as if she'd lost her wits. "I've got to talk to you about something really important!" he hissed, under the hubbub of everyone's conversations. "Aunt Mildred has stolen my photo of the Long-tailed Pink Polka-dotted Home-wrecking Cuckoo! She and the rest of S.L.A.Y. must've been after it. Mum said she thought poachers were after her, remember? Julius Rapax must want the cuckoo – the letters give S.L.A.Y. the location, and the photo now means they can be sure of identifying it." He shook his head in sorrow. "Which is why Mum said keep it safe. Now S.L.A.Y. will be able to get their ten million!"

Imogen looked at Danny, wide-eyed. "Oh, Danny, that's really horrible. But they've still got your mum to contend with. She might be able to outsmart them! Anyway, as awful as it sounds, we've got even more pressing concerns. We've got to think about you now. We've got to break the hex! I'll tell you la—"

She was cut off by a poke in the ribs from Aunt Mildred. Imogen glared at her.

They were all filing into a pew near the front of the church, Dad on the end of the row, Aunt Mildred beside him, then Danny between her and Imogen. Danny spotted Chopper Chowdhury in the row across the aisle.

He slid down and hastily faced the front.

The imposing figure of the bridegroom, the bully's older brother, stood with hands clasped in front of him, facing the altar. Big Mal's smart suit crackled stiffly as he looked around and inspected the crowd now sitting expectantly behind him. His eyes narrowed suspiciously when he saw Danny; clearly he was trying to remember where he'd seen him before…

Danny felt his heart begin to race. At that moment organ music swelled to fill the church and the bride started down the aisle on the arm of her father. Big Mal

172

turned to face the front, and Danny's bacon was saved for the time being.

Vicar Nannish droned on, hymns were sung, bible passages read and Danny and Imogen exchanged nervous looks. Each second that passed was a second closer to something truly awful happening.

Imogen leaned over and hissed into Danny's ear. "No sign of Smurth –" That was when she noticed Danny's face had an oddly glazed look about it. "Oh, no," she whispered hoarsely. She shook him, but to no avail.

"If any man can show just cause," Vicar Nannish intoned over the heads of Blodwyn and Big Mal, addressing the audience beyond, "why they may not lawfully be joined together, let him now speak, or else hereafter forever hold his peace."

Danny shot to his feet as if he'd sat on a bed of nails. "I PROTEST!" he yelled at the top of his voice, waving his arms about.

There were cries of shock and surprise all around the church. Everyone turned to look at him. "Sit down!" Dad hissed angrily from the end of the pew. But Danny remained on his feet.

"Well?" the vicar said coldly, recognizing Danny. "And it had better be good." There was muted laughter at this.

The hexed Danny continued, oblivious to the mayhem he was causing. "The bridegroom's excessive snoring will ruin the marriage, your worshipfulness!" Big Mal spun round, murder in his eyes.

There was a gale of laughter from the congregation so unexpected that Vicar Nannish found himself reminding them all of the sanctity of the place and the occasion. "As God would forgive this young man here in this holy place, I think so should we all," he went on. "Sit down, Danny, and we'll continue with the ceremony. Now, where were we?"

But Danny could hear nothing above the victorious, raucous cackle of the Hobblegob, magnified many times louder than ever before.

Outside the church after the ceremony, Dad was seething with silent anger. There was an awful hollow feeling inside Danny. As Imogen squeezed Danny's hand,

Aunt Mildred spoke, the words dripping from her tongue like honey. "Terry, if I may say something?" Dad nodded curtly.

"I've spoken to Blods and Mal," she said, gesturing towards the happy couple standing on a distant knoll having their formal photographs taken. "They've seen the funny side of it. Put Danny's disgraceful performance down to mere high jinks. Apparently he called them names last weekend too after he'd insulted the vicar. But they don't want anything to spoil their special day. They said he's obviously going through a difficult *spell*, but don't want to *bar* him from coming," she continued, her eyes glittering malevolently at Danny as she stressed the two doom-laden words. "They've asked that we put all this silliness behind us and come and enjoy the wedding reception. The Pink Pig's doing the catering. There's spare ribs – your favourite," she wheedled her husband.

Mr. Cloke looked surprised at his wife's magnanimous reaction. Mollified, he found himself agreeing to go to the reception. But a paralysing terror had filled Danny and Imogen during Aunt Mildred's speech. They felt sure that Danny was about to meet his doom.

Chapter 12

A Fiery Reception

THE RECEPTION WAS in a marquee in the grounds of a small castle. The wedding party was seated at the top table, facing their guests, who sat at dozens of smaller, circular tables, candlelight flickering in the centre of each one. Along one side of the marquee was a long table stacked high with unopened wedding presents.

On the opposite side of the tent a magnificent white three-tiered wedding cake was displayed on a silver platter. A great ceremonial silver knife with a white ribbon tied to it lay waiting to cut the cake.

Everyone had finished dessert and people were beginning to get up and mingle at different tables. Blodwyn drifted past, giving Danny a nasty stare. Vicar Nannish was with her. He too glanced over, shaking his head sadly. Opposite him, Danny glimpsed Aunt Mildred. She was watching him with a look of amusement, a smile playing across her lips. Dad sat, round-shouldered, at her side. Hearing his name mentioned, Danny looked around and saw Chopper Chowdhury at a nearby table, talking to his big brother and slapping a fist into his open palm.

"Oh, no," groaned Imogen. "Smurthwaite's just arrived."

"This is the worst day of my entire life," Danny said to Imogen. "And that's not even counting Aunt Mildred finding the photo. It's like waiting for a time bomb to go off."

"It's awful," agreed Imogen. "But come with me, Danny. There might be something we can do."

As Danny and Imogen climbed to their feet, a portly waiter wearing a rather grand cummerbund politely asked them if they were looking forward to the fireworks. "These aren't any old bangers," the man added pleasantly. "They're the latest fireworks from China. Very expensive."

"Danny," Imogen whispered as the waiter walked away and went outside. "Your Aunt Mildred mentioned this to my mum. This is the chance we've been waiting for, and it could be our last."

As they slipped out of the marquee's entrance, Imogen went on, "Listen. Just after detention I copied the hex letter with Tarquin's Exact Replica Parchment Copier. It worked perfectly – even the underlined words are identical. Hey presto! Two hex letters!"

"Great," said Danny as they headed down a grassy slope with a cow pasture in the distance in the valley below. "But how will two letters help?"

"Like this: we let Aunt Mildred think she's got the original," Imogen continued, "I'm going to give her the copy in a minute. Only she won't know it's a copy – hopefully. After that she won't be worrying about lighting fires that'll undo the Zero Hex, will she? So we're going to try and trick her into burning the *real* hex letter! I know it's going to be difficult, but it's our only chance."

"It's worth a try," said Danny. "But where's the real hex letter?"

Imogen smiled. "It's in my left-hand pocket," she said, patting it. "The copy's in the right-hand one. This is the plan. We've got to stuff the original letter inside one of the fireworks. And then somehow get Aunt Mildred to light it."

Faint hope flickered in Danny's eyes. "Oh, Imogen, if only we can make it work!"

Halfway down the hill the pair came across the friendly waiter lining up fireworks for the display. "Careful there, kids," he called out. "You shouldn't really be down here, you know."

As Danny engaged the waiter in conversation about the amazing Chinese fireworks, distracting him for a moment, Imogen crept behind him and lifted the crackling red paper from the top of a firework the size of a bucket. Screwing up the original hex letter, she forced the ball of paper inside, right next to the firework's long fuse. She pressed the red paper back into place and straightened up quickly. Just in the nick of time.

"Admiring Big Bertha were you, Missy?" the waiter said, turning round. "That's the highlight of the evening, the last one in the display. People in the next village will think war's broken out," he finished with a toothy grin.

"I heard the bride say she hoped you'd pick out one of the guests to light Big Bertha," Imogen said, with sudden inspiration.

"Did she now?" said the waiter and put his hand to his chin.

As Danny and Imogen marched up the hill and back into the marquee, they agreed that so far fortune seemed to be smiling on them, for once. "I heard Aunt Mildred say she's picking up the bill for all this. The waiter might choose her as guest of honour," Danny said hopefully. "But she'll still be on the lookout for anything like that," he added.

"I know, but it's got to be easier if she thinks she's got the real hex letter. Stay here, Danny." With that, Imogen marched up to Aunt Mildred, who was now standing with Smurthwaite.

Danny watched open-mouthed as she said softly to Aunt Mildred, "When you call the police with these ridiculous accusations about me being in your hotel suite last night, I'm going to show them this!" She produced the copy of the hex letter with a flourish.

Smurthwaite snatched the letter from Imogen's hand, folded it up and handed it to Aunt Mildred. Within the blink of an eye, she dropped it into her handbag and the clasp snapped shut with the force of a piranha's teeth.

As Danny looked on, he saw that Imogen's face was brilliantly feigning absolute devastation.

"I suggest you both have another plate of ice cream," said Aunt Mildred, grinning wickedly. "It might be Danny's last."

When everyone had assembled in the chill night air outside the marquee, glasses in hand and whispering excitedly, the fireworks began. As the first great orange blooms filled the sky, two waiters moved among the crowd, carrying between them the magnificent three-tiered wedding cake on its silver platter, and a third waiter was offering forks and little white plates.

Danny and Imogen were surprised that despite their increasing sense of dread, they felt a few brief moments of joy, so spectacular were the fireworks. Red circles grew ever larger in the air, like advancing shields. A hundred shimmering rainbows arched across the sky, and something that looked alarmingly like a great silver scythe whistled over the heads of the crowd with a shrill scream.

As he watched the show, an idea formed in Danny's mind. "I know how we can get Aunt Mildred to light the firework, Imogen!" he said, trembling with excitement, as a shower of turquoise fell from the sky. "You just wait and see."

"And now, ladies and gentlemen," roared the waiter, "we come to the highlight of the evening. Big Bertha! No, she's not a dancing girl, but this," and he indicated the bucket-like firework at his feet. "I will pick one member of the crowd to come forward and light it."

"Me! Me! Me!" shouted Danny, pushing to the front of the crowd to put his plan into action.

"All right then, young man," said the waiter. "The honour is yours."

Danny stepped forwards.

"Stop!"

The voice was Aunt Mildred's. This was precisely the reaction Danny had expected. He knew how much she would hate him getting even the tiniest bit of enjoyment out of anything.

"Ladies and gentlemen," Aunt Mildred pronounced, throwing her arms wide, trying to appear magnanimous. "Forgive me for sounding so churlish, but I really don't think that Danny deserves the honour. He behaved poorly in church today. If I may beg the audience's indulgence, I would be honoured if I could do it."

"Oh, please do, Mildred," Blodwyn called out. "You've made the day so special."

"Mildred, the honour is yours then," said the waiter with a smile.

Danny scowled at Aunt Mildred but inside his heart was turning somersaults. The man handed Mildred the box of matches. Yessss! thought Danny. Please let this work. Please please *please*! An expectant hush had fallen over the crowd.

The match flowered with flame and Danny watched

on, hardly daring to breathe. The firework's fuse fizzed loudly and began glowing bright orange.

Then, several things happened at once.

As the waiters approached carrying the wedding cake, Danny was suddenly tripped forwards, and he and the waiters' legs became tangled. The huge cake with its silver platter went sailing into the air. Danny stumbled to the ground, hitting his head as he did so, and everyone within a radius of ten metres was covered from head to toe in cake, cream and icing.

As the screaming began, and blackness consumed him, the last thing Danny saw was Chopper Chowdhury leering victoriously at him as he pulled his foot back in...

When Danny's eyes swam back into focus some moments later, he found himself lying on his back, staring up at the sky. It took him several seconds to remember what had happened. But he was still baffled as to why everyone around him was holding their nose, eyes streaming, looks of horror and disgust etched across their faces.

"Cloke's let off a stink bomb," Chopper Chowdhury was bellowing, shaking Big Mal's arm.

Had Chopper let off a stink bomb, Danny wondered vaguely, and was he blaming it on him in retaliation for the drawing-pin incident?

Big Mal's eyes narrowed as he studied Danny's prone form. The same young hooligan who had taunted him a week ago, and ruined his marriage vows, was now responsible for covering his guests in wedding cake and, apparently, had also let off a stink bomb. Big Mal wanted revenge. "Get him!" he roared. Chopper had a gleeful look in his eye as he leaped into action with his older brother.

"Danny!" screamed Imogen, instantly at his side, and pulling him to his feet. "Get up! The Chowdhurys!"

At these words Danny's disorientation left him as quickly as it had arrived. He and Imogen ran for the exit, where Aunt Mildred and Smurthwaite tried to make a grab at them. But Danny's dad got in the way, allowing them to evade capture and head off at top speed down the grassy slope towards the narrow lane that led into the village.

"Come back at once!" shrieked Aunt Mildred, hopping with rage. "This wasn't meant to happen! Why did you let them get away, Terry?"

Danny's dad shrugged absently. "Might not have been him. Remember the patch, Mildred?"

The lumbering Chowdhurys soon gave up the chase and returned to the wreckage of the wedding reception.

"Imogen," Danny gasped as they came to a stop, and he clutched at a stitch in his side. "The firework was our last hope, and now it's gone."

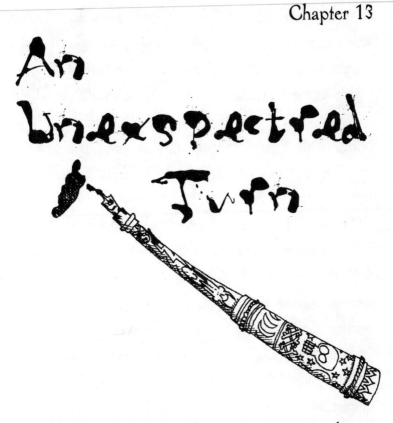

Chapter 13

An Unexspected Turn

"**B**UT WE'VE DONE IT, DANNY! We've beaten the Zero Hex!" Imogen was jigging around with excitement, her eyes shining.

"What?" Danny said, gaping at her.

"You're finally unhexed," Imogen said, coming to a breathless stop. She shook both of his hands at once.

"You mean Aunt Mildred still lit the firework," Danny said, agog, "with all that cake flying about, and Chopper tripping me up, and setting off his stink bomb?"

Imogen grinned at him. "Yes, she did. She'd already lit it. And do you know what? I don't think there was a stink bomb at all. That disgusting smell was the fumes of the magical, horrible hex ink – all those poisonous words finally going up in flames!"

Danny whooped with joy, and grabbing Imogen's hands, spun her round and round in an ecstatic whirl. When they eventually slowed down, Danny took in their surroundings. "Look where we are," he said. "The cemetery. Shall we go and tell Cyril we've won?"

"Yes," said Imogen, her eyes alight with happiness.

The gates of the Under-the-Sod Cemetery gave a protesting groan as Imogen pushed them open. They hurried inside.

"He might not actually appear," said Danny as they picked their way through the tombstones. "But I'm going to tell his gravestone, anyway. You won't think I'm going crazy, will you?"

"Of course not! After all that's happened, talking to a

block of marble in a graveyard seems positively normal!"
Danny grinned at her.

When they reached Cyril Clegg's gravestone, Danny reached out and touched it. The stone seemed to come to life beneath his fingers, and an instant later the familiar form of Cyril appeared, gliding effortlessly out of the marble and floating in midair before them.

"Cyril!" Danny cried, elated. "You're here! Am I glad to see you."

"Danny!" said Imogen. "Stop messing about."

"No, no, really," said Danny, pointing. "He's here...he's... You can't see him, can you?"

Imogen looked crestfallen. "You're not messing about, are you? Oh, how disappointing. But, Cyril, h-hello anyway," she added, peering about and seeing nothing but thin air. "I think you're great, too."

"Hold her hand, dear boy," said Cyril, "or she won't be able to *ear-trumpet* me either. When you take her hand, she will see and hear what you can. I will explain everything in a moment."

Danny looked at Imogen. "Cyril says I'm to hold your hand, and then you'll see the same as me."

Imogen thrust her hand into his. A moment later, she cried out in surprise. "Cyril!"

"*Enchanterous* to meet you, Miss Falconer," Cyril said, performing a polite bow in midair. "The *measure's* all *pine*. Anyway, Danny, let's get *bound* to *dizziness*. You've defeated the Zero Hex. But did you ever ask yourself *why* a *disgusterous* Hobblegob would do such a thing?"

Feeling a little deflated that Cyril already knew his good news, Danny shook his head. He felt his mouth going dry.

Cyril looked grim. "Because something happened to you, that was a wholly *unexspectred* turn; something that has the most *swazzling* significance to the mortal world and also to all of Forever, as you will soon come to realize."

Danny was suddenly afraid of what he was going to hear.

"Listen carefully," Cyril continued. "Forever has always had three spirit forms and three realms. They are the Haloes of Paradise, the Hobblegobs of Gloom and the Spectres of the Waiting Rooms. I think you're already aware of this. But now the situation has changed. Now there's a fourth form...*you*."

"ME?" said Danny. He and Imogen looked at each other, confused. "What do you mean by that?"

"You're the world's first ever living ghost, Danny – and probably its last. You see when you came into my waiting room the first time and broke the Hero Hex, you took a little piece of Forever back into the world with you. Saint Bernard didn't realize until too late, of course. The Hobblegobs were highly suspicious, saying Saint Bernard had done it on purpose, trying to invent a new type of spirit that might turn out to be a powerful enemy against them. That's why Neville Neville agreed so readily to Zero Hex you. Spirits aren't normally allowed to get involved with mere humans, you know, not even Hobblegobs."

"I see," said Danny. "So the Hobblegobs hate me, is that it?" This didn't sound like good news. "Well, things could've turned out worse I suppose. I might've ended up behind bars and looking forward to a life of crime; that is if I hadn't ended up dead from the beating the Chowdhurys were about to dish out, that is."

"Actually, sometimes you will be dead," Cyril said blithely.

"WHAT!" yelled Danny.

"It's not as *gruesifying* as it sounds," Cyril said, trying to placate him. "Occasionally, your ghost form will slip out of your body. There will be no warning, and you'll have very little control over it. It can't be helped, I'm afraid. During these times your *earthsome* body will be *medicinally* dead. You'll be as helpless as a newborn *blubbaby*. But you're going to have to be very careful. It could cause a *skied highbrow* or two if you're found dead during maths class or suchlike. Downright dangerous if your ghostly form slips its *worldbound* moorings while you're crossing a busy road. You'd be dead twice in ten seconds – only the second time would be permanent."

Danny swallowed nervously. "It all sounds horrible. How will I know what to do if I suddenly become a ghost?"

"It'll be just like being me," said Cyril soothingly. "And all you've got to remember is that where there's no solid form, thoughts are everything. Anyway, haven't you had any *peepy* inklings about your *ghosthood* during these past few weeks?" Cyril asked.

"Er, no," said Danny uncertainly.

"Well, for a start," Cyril said, waving his hands impatiently, "you can see Hobblegobs, dear boy. It's completely unheard of. You've made them very *jitterous*," he added with a mischievous chuckle.

"I thought that was part of the Zero Hex," said Danny. "And anyway, it was only one Hobblegob."

"Two, actually," said Cyril. "My *charmful* wife Malicia's been dead these past twenty years and took to Hobblegobblery like a *duck-billed jellypus* to water. Her bones are rattling at the opposite end of the churchyard."

"But I saw her at the S.L.A.Y. meeting…?"

"You were the only one to have any idea that she was there," said Cyril. "You didn't see Malicia, did you, Imogen?" She shook her head. "Anyway, the *crustulescent* Malicia's been doing a little bit of quiet spy work and you've been giving her the fright of her death, apparently, when you kept popping up! She thought you'd been sent to spy on her!" Cyril roared with laughter, finishing with an asthmatic wheeze and a cough.

"Nor was it part of the Zero Hex when you shifted Chopper's drawing pin from Imogen's seat to his own. Remember how you felt dizzy with anger? Actually, your ghostly part left your body for a couple of seconds, and performed the switch without you consciously realizing it! And what about when you could see the hex pen in Aunt Mildred's suite and Imogen couldn't? Or even the fact that Imogen can't see me without your assistance?" Cyril grinned. "But I'm definitely taking the credit for *repleating* the 'Cyril Spectre Spells Magic' patch back on your jeans," he replied. "A *misterstroke!*"

"But what about Neville Neville?" asked Imogen. "Is he still a danger to Danny?"

Cyril thrust his chin out, looking feisty. "Not while I'm around. I'm more than a match for him." He ducked about in the air, imitating a boxer. "I'll parry. I'll give him the old *heft look*. Pow-pow! I came, I saw, I conjured!"

Danny and Imogen were laughing at his antics when Cyril suddenly became serious again. "Ahem," he cleared his throat, looking slightly embarrassed. "Actually I'm not allowed to interfere or I'll get in *icky, treacly tread double*. But I can tell you that Neville Neville, or Cat O' Nine Tails as he likes to call himself these days, was a truly *disgusterous* man. He was my best friend when I was Cyril Clegg. He lived for a while in a large town in the state of *Meatysoda*, where he opened up a store called Addictive Pizza 4 Kidz. When he left, even the smallest ten-year-old child in that town weighed a *blubberfying* hundred and ten kilos. I didn't *sky a highbrow* when I learned that this was the Hobblegob *guiltiponsiful* for your Zero Hex."

"Now we know where Aunt Mildred learned all her tricks," said Imogen.

"The Hobblegobs truly fear the power a living ghost may possess," Cyril continued. "Even the Haloes fear what may happen if you turn *nasterous*. And the Spectres are just plain jealous, muttering that they had to wait until they were dead to do any haunting. You are unique! And you're both going to have to find a way of using that uniqueness to defeat Aunt Mildred and S.L.A.Y. ..."

"What can we do," asked Danny, "now that Aunt Mildred's got the cuckoo photo?"

Cyril frowned. "I don't know. But you'll have to come up with something. She's been *sneaksifying* your letters for years, following the progress of your mother's search. It's the real reason Aunt Mildred married your father. Right now she is *ratslinking* towards her hotel suite, clutching her prize. Then she will fly out to Parvatelli, the capital of the island of Bella Vista. S.L.A.Y. has spent many years *blunderbussing* about looking for the cuckoo, and people have died - including Alfie Stringfellow - and all because they'd been promised ten million for it. Now she has the photo she thinks they'll be able to capture it with the new-*fangulous* widget cage, courtesy of your father."

"Does he have any idea?"

"None," said Cyril. "But that *sleasel* Julius Rapax has been systematically removing animals from the wild for as long as anyone can remember. I'll bet you've never seen a Caspian tiger or a Barbary lion: all because of him. It's his pet project, just as *sleepcrashing* children with Cyril Clegg books is Miss Snodgrass's. In a world run by S.L.A.Y. there will no birdsong, no animals, no music, no books – no dreams! Just grey highways interspersed with great chimneys and everyone *enslayed*."

Danny stared in horror at Cyril. "We've got to stop them! The cuckoo's my mum's life's work."

"I *wishous* you all the delicious luck that I can. You'll change the world, and even Forever, one day, Danny," said Cyril. "But come now. My time here is finished. So it's goodbye again. Never give up hope. And remember, everyone's memories will have been severely *tampstered* with. They will have forgotten a great deal," he added, laughing. "Because humans aren't allowed to recall their *brushes and combs* with the spirit world. You, however, are no longer *extirely* human, Danny. Let that give you courage in your future *prattles* with S.L.A.Y. So Imogen, goodbye. Goodbye, dear boy."

"You will always be my greatest hero, Cyril Spectre," said Danny.

"Mine too, Cyril," Imogen added.

"One day I may well be saying that you're my greatest heroes, too," said Cyril and he vanished within the gravestone.

Danny and Imogen were left staring wistfully at his grave when, all of a sudden, something swooped out of the darkness. They cowered on the grass as an evil cackling laugh filled the air. The malevolent form of the Hobblegob, Neville Neville, rose above them, his sharp teeth glinting and his red eyes staring. Suddenly he lunged at Danny. Moments later, Imogen found herself next to Danny's prone form. He was lying on the ground, his eyes staring sightlessly upwards.

Chapter 14

A Spell Behind Bars

AT FIRST DANNY WAS only aware of Neville Neville's ringing laughter. As his eyes adjusted themselves to the gloom, he found himself in a low, vaulted chamber piled high with spectral debris and filth, dominated in the middle by a square cage, hovering in midair. Its walls, floor and ceiling were comprised of thick, spectral, tubular bars of mist.

"Welcome to my grave," cackled Neville Neville, his mouth twisting horribly. "I'd like to thank you for coming to the graveyard. It saved me the trouble of having to find you." Gesturing, the evil creature continued, "This cage took me to Gloom, where I was turned into a Hobblegob. And now I have plucked your ghost from your human form, it will do the same to you."

Shocked, Danny glanced down at himself. He saw that he was as insubstantial as a wisp of steam and glowing strangely. "We beat the Zero Hex fair and square!" Danny yelled.

"If Saint Bernard can meddle in the affairs of humans," Neville Neville roared, "then so can I! You are a danger to the whole spirit world, Danny Cloke, so prepare to meet your doom!" The Hobblegob opened the door to the cage and flung Danny inside.

The barred door closed again with a resounding slam. Although they looked formless, Danny found himself – that is, his spirit form – unable to move back through the bars. The Hobblegob leaped onto a great shimmering silver lever that was beside the cage. It gave a mighty squeal and jerked and swayed.

An enormous trapdoor fell open with a doom-laden boom and Danny had his first glimpse of the sheer scale of Forever. Below his feet, through the bars of the cage, he could see a dizzying number of identical cages, moving relentlessly downwards, all attached to wires, like cable cars. Each cage was transporting the occupant of a grave to their fate in Gloom.

Looking into the great yawning expanse of Forever, Danny saw a sign that said: Gateway to Gloom. Further down was another sign, this one proclaiming, Slain Lane: low-chief Hobblegobs only.

Neville Neville cast a mocking eye over Danny. "It takes ten years to get to Gloom's reception area. You may have defeated a human, but you won't escape a Hobblegob's spell behind bars!"

Danny gasped as the cage he was in gave a sudden jerk and started to descend down – down – down into the abyss that was teeming with other cages. A great roaring filled the air; the thunderous rattling of the cages' descent mingled with wails of misery and fear.

Neville Neville flew beside the plummeting cable car, laughing mockingly at him. "Danny Cloke, the aberration to the natural order of things, will be no more," he said in a voice as cold as an ice age. "If the S.A.I.N.T.s were planning anything, it doesn't matter now."

As Danny looked on, wide-eyed with panic, the Hobblegob swept his arms majestically in front of his face, his hands cupped together. Colourful balls of scintillating light hissed and sizzled as they danced about the Hobblegob's fingertips. Thrusting both arms in Danny's direction, Neville Neville fired dozens of these strange bubbles at him.

In the split second that they approached him, in a blaze of colour and noise, Danny saw that they all contained a single moving image of one of Danny's nightmares, his waking fears and most shameful moments. He barely ducked in time, and they sizzled, screaming, past his head. The Hobblegob cupped his hands again, and another wave of bubbles exploded around Danny. Finally, one hit him in the face. Immediately, an old nightmare consumed him like a blinding burst of emptiness and night. Suddenly he was seven years old again, and his mother had vanished without even saying goodbye. "Oh, no. No! No!" he cried.

Danny was blasted on all sides by image-filled bubbles. He tried to conjure up some good memories, but he felt lost in a world of nightmares. Just as darkness threatened to swallow him completely, Danny's mind clutched hold of a beautiful, shimmering thought. He imagined his mum, out in the jungle, looking up through the canopy of the trees and watching in awe as the magnificent Long-tailed Pink Polka-dotted Home-wrecking Cuckoo soared overhead into the sunlight.

Then, Danny hugged this thought to himself, and as he clung onto it, something remarkable happened. The image-filled bubbles that Neville Neville was throwing out seemed to strike an invisible shield around Danny and the bubbles ricocheted back towards the Hobblegob. They smashed through the bars of the cage and struck the Hobblegob in an almighty explosion of noise and colour.

The wicked creature screamed in agony and then seemed to implode, all the dark matter that was Neville Neville melting to a single point, which then disappeared.

Then, Danny felt himself being borne upwards, through the smashed bars of the cage towards a tiny patch of light far above. A pair of mighty wings was beating and Danny saw flashes of glorious pink-flecked feathers.

It was the Long-tailed Pink Polka-dotted Home-wrecking Cuckoo.

Danny's heart soared with every thrust of its wings.

Opening his eyes, Danny blinked in the moonlight. Imogen's face swam slowly into focus, and he saw that he was lying beside Cyril's grave. "Danny Cloke! I've been frightened to death!" she said, looking ashen. "Oh, you've made it. Oh, thank goodness. I really thought you were a goner," she gabbled.

Danny, still feeling dazed and raw, but strangely elated, did his best to describe to Imogen the sheer wickedness of Neville Neville, the spectral cage and the awful, awesome depths of the realm of Gloom.

"How on earth did you manage to escape?" asked Imogen, staring at him, wide-eyed with horror.

"Well, I don't really know how it happened," admitted Danny, "but just as I thought it was curtains, this wonderful image of the Long-tailed Pink Polka-dotted

Home-wrecking Cuckoo burst into my head. It was so beautiful, and I felt so powerful, and it filled me with hope. It acted as a sort of shield and deflected all the Hobblegob's bubbles back onto itself, destroying it, and then I was soaring upwards, on the back of this enormous, magnificent bird and then…well, and then I was back here again. I don't really understand. The cuckoo was so big…"

"Well," said Imogen, "remember what Cyril said about thoughts being everything when there's no solid form? Anyway, you're obviously a very powerful ghost if you can defeat that evil Hobblegob."

"I guess so," said Danny, looking doubtful.

"Of course you are, Danny. Remember Cyril's words: you'll change the world. I'm sure we can beat Aunt Mildred if only we can learn to harness your powers."

Danny didn't really want to think about Aunt Mildred and her evil organization right now, but he knew one thing. "We've got to save the cuckoo," he told Imogen. "It saved my life, and now I have to do the same for it. Tomorrow, we'll have our first official anti-S.L.A.Y. meeting. But come on, let's go back to my place now."